The Daughters of Time, Book 2

The Secrets of the Cottage

Some things go bump...

C.S. Kjar

C.S. Kjar

Editor: JoEllen Claypool
Cover Designed by jimmygibbs
Proofreading by John Buchanan and Julie Martin

Available in eBook and Paperback

Paperback ISBN: 978-0-9985897-4-9
Digital ISBN: 978-0-9985897-5-6

http://cskjar.com

This book is dedicated to my sister, Julie, for displaying strength during her troubles. She faced her fears, overcame them, and is stronger for it. I admire her for that. Women everywhere need that kind of strength.

Chapter 1

The Neighbors

An unearthly moaning floated with the breeze that ruffled Estelle Gribnitz's hair as she stood on the back patio of her Florida beach condo. In the light of the full moon, she stared at the white stone cottage of a crazy woman who died a year ago. The lights inside the cottage flickered on and off like a child was playing with them. The hair on the back of Estelle's neck stood on end as dreadful moans and sounds from the house reached her ears. A shudder moved through her.

Estelle held her cell phone above her head to record the eerie sounds. In her many calls to report the disturbances, the sheriff told her no one lived there, but she knew better. Something was alive there. Focusing more on the cottage, she held her phone steady, its video app recording the eerie sounds drifting toward her patio. If the sheriff didn't believe her stories, he couldn't deny the video. Someone or something was still living in that house, turning the lights on and off all night and screeching like a tortured cat.

"Estelle!" Her husband Frank shouted so suddenly it caused Estelle to jump and nearly drop her phone. Behind her, the screen door creaked as it was opened. "What are you doing out here?" he asked.

Estelle quickly stopped the recording. She shot Frank

a look she hoped would zap him a little. "Hush your mouth! I'm trying to record the sounds from the haunted house. You're messing it up." She turned away from him and started recording again as a loud yell came from the cottage. "The sheriff has to believe a video," she muttered.

Shuffling across the gritty patio in his bare feet and shorts, Frank flopped into a lawn chair and released his own moan. "That place is not haunted. It's a party house for kids. There's no such thing as ghosts."

The oft-heard words forced Estelle to roll her eyes. Not a believer in ghosts either, the sights and sounds coming from the cottage were changing her mind. College-kid parties involved music. There was no music coming across the grassy space. Just eerie, blood-curdling noises. Maybe ghosts did exist. All she needed was proof.

Not wanting to argue with Frank, she conceded. "If you're convinced it's a party, why don't you call the police again. Make them go run those scoundrels out of there. The noise is disturbing our peace and quiet."

Through the screen door, they heard their front doorbell ring. With a grunt of effort, Frank got up. "I'll go get that. I bet it's Charlie and Kathy coming over to visit."

As he passed behind Estelle, she told him, "Wipe off your feet. I swept the carpet today, and I don't want any more sand tracked in."

Giving a grunt of compliance, Frank wiped his bare feet with an emoted flair and went in.

Giving up on her video recording, Estelle put her phone in the pocket of her capris and waited for their neighbors to join them on the patio. The lights in the cottage flickered once, then went off. The eerie noises ceased, leaving only the night chirps of the insects and the voices and footsteps of Frank, Charlie, and Kathy to fill the air.

Kathy came rushing out to the patio. "Did you hear that racket over there?" she asked as she stood next to Estelle, facing the now-silent cottage. "Charlie called the sheriff. I think he's tired of us calling him. Said he might send someone over to see what's going on, but he doubted they'd find anything."

Estelle pulled her phone from her pocket and waved it in front of her friend's face. "What he needs is proof of what we're talking about. I'm going to video it and show it to him. He can't refute solid evidence."

A pat on the back from Kathy boosted her confidence in her plan. She'd show that sheriff she wasn't the crazy one. Something unnatural was going on.

A shrill screech came from the direction of the cottage, causing the women to jump and let out a howl of fright. Estelle's heart hammered in her chest as she raced at full speed toward the patio door. Kathy hit the door at the same time as Estelle, causing the full-figured women to hit the sides of the door and stumble inside. Leaving sand on the carpet behind her, Estelle faltered to the sofa before collapsing. Kathy went to her knees beside the door.

Their husbands stood staring at the spectacle, holding their drinks in stunned silence. They looked at each other, lifted their glasses in salute, and took a sip.

"I can't take it anymore!" Estelle cried out with the agony of someone teetering on the edge of mental stability. "Every night. Lights. Blinking. Sounds. Eerie." She paused to clutch her chest to make sure her heart was still beating. She rose and went to Frank, burying her face in his ample chest. "And during the full moons, it gets worse. Otherworldish sounds come from that supposedly deserted house. Forget the police, I'm calling a priest. That house is full of demons!" She shook a fist in the direction of the cottage.

Frank put his drink down and guided her back to the sofa.

Charlie set his drink down too. He went to help Kathy off the floor and onto the sofa beside Estelle.

Kathy reached over to hang on to her trembling friend. "That's a good idea, Estelle. In the morning, we'll call a priest. He'll know what to do."

"You don't need no priest," barked Frank. Charlie came up behind him nodding. "A bunch of kids are down there partying their stupid heads off. The sheriff will take care of them. Quit imagining this supernatural stuff. There's no such thing!"

Estelle looked away and pursed her lips. "Those sounds are not earthly. They are from beyond."

Kathy nodded.

"Beyond what?" Frank held his arms wide, inviting an answer to fill them.

Charlie snorted. "Don't waste your breath, Frank. They're feeding each other's fears. It's more cool" –he made quotation signs with his fingers as he said the word– "to imagine something unnatural than it is to use common sense." He and Frank laughed as they went out on the patio.

Kathy let out an exasperated sound. "Those over-bloated bigheads! Too blind to see!" She gave Estelle a sideways hug.

Estelle got up and paced in her immaculately kept, but now sandy, living room. "Maybe I'm going crazy, but it seems to me since that Time woman died," she stabbed the air with her finger, "that place has been haunted."

She stopped pacing and took in a quick breath. "I wonder if she's the one causing the problems. I mean, she was always friendly to me, but I wasn't overly friendly to her. She seemed so odd that I didn't want to be around her. She must be holding a grudge and getting me back." A cry of anguish bolted from her lips as she wrung her hands. "She's haunting me from her house!"

The front doorbell resonated through the living room like a thunderclap from a clear blue sky. Estelle and Kathy jerked like they had been electrocuted, emitting soft screams.

"Must be the police," Charlie said calmly to Frank as they came inside, tracking more sand across Estelle's carpet. Ignoring the two women on the sofa, he continued, "I told them to come over here." He followed Frank to the door to let the lone officer in. Customary greetings were exchanged as the officer stepped into the living room.

The middle-aged Officer Glen Stanus stood in front of the sofa with his hands on his utility belt. "Nice to see you again, Frank. Charlie." He nodded to both ladies. "Estelle. Kathy. That party still going on at the crazy woman's house?"

Estelle leapt up, her arm started flailing with a mind of its own as it pointed out the patio door. "That crazy woman's house is alive! It's haunting me with the moans and screams coming out of it." She stood there shaking until Frank came and steadied her. "It's haunted," she said. "People..." she glared up at Frank, "...think I'm crazy, but I'm not. Go over there and take Frank with you. You'll see there's something spooky going on there."

She saw a flash of fear in the officer's eyes before he looked down at his feet. Officer Stanus pointed toward the patio door with raised eyebrows. Given permission to go, he stepped outside with the foursome on his heels.

They stood silent, listening for any noise coming from the direction of the cottage. Only bugs, frogs, surf, and distant traffic were heard. They waited a little longer. Still nothing unusual.

Estelle wrung her hands. Why wouldn't the lights blink like they'd done for the past hour? Why wouldn't sounds come from the cottage now that she had witnesses?

"Believe me," she begged, "eerie sounds were coming from that cottage right before you got here. Tell him, Frank." She pushed Frank forward.

Frank held up his hands in surrender. "Don't involve me in this. If I hear anything funny, I turn down my hearing aid, so it doesn't bother me."

Estelle had suspected as much. His device made it too easy for him to have selective hearing. A discussion about it would come after their company left.

Desperate to find proof of what she heard, she felt in her pocket. "I recorded the sounds." She pulled out her phone and started the last video. She handed it to Officer Stanus. He stared at the black screen, then held it up to his ear. Listening for a minute, he shook his head and gave the phone back to her.

Estelle's head fell to her chest. She took her phone back and stuffed it in her pocket.

Kathy came to her rescue. "I'm her witness. I heard them too. Screams and loud moans. You never heard such."

Officer Stanus waved them off. "I'll go over there again to make sure no one's around. It's time to call the owners and tell them to come take care of things. I'll suggest that in my report. If there's nothing else you need from me, good evening to you." He left the foursome on the patio peering into the quiet darkness.

Keeping his strong façade in place until he reached his cruiser, Glen Stanus got in and grabbed his cell phone. "Call Sarge on mobile," he told the electronic secretary. "And hurry!"

Drawing in a slow breath, he tried to calm his pounding heart. So many butterflies swirled in his stomach he almost coughed one up. The sound of his sergeant's voice answering the phone didn't calm him much. "Sir, it's that crazy woman's house again. The full moon has stirred up the phantoms or demons or whatever is there."

"Not surprising," the sergeant said with a yawn.

Glen pumped his fist a time or two, hoping to find the courage to ask what he wanted to ask. "Do I have to go over there? We know I won't find anything, so why bother?"

"Did you tell them you would go?"

With his eyes squeezed together tightly, Glen let out a mouse-toned yes.

The police sergeant was quiet for a moment. "Just do a drive-by. If you can't see anything from your cruiser, leave. You don't have to get out to look around."

Glen's heart slowed its pace as he said, "Thanks, Sarge. Heading over there now."

He hung up and started his car. He drove the now-familiar route to the haunted house. He'd been there several times before. So had the other patrolmen at the station. All of them had had unexplainable things happen while they were there. Lights going on and off. Papers flying out of the glove box. Strange voices coming out of the air. Being pushed around by invisible forces. The list went on.

He'd faced drunks and crooks, been to domestic disputes, and cleaned up after car wrecks, but nothing scared him like checking this house did. Dread almost overpowered him as he turned into the driveway of the cottage. As he pulled up by the porch, the lights blinked on and off again. A bead of sweat trickled down his brow. He mentally thanked the sergeant for permission to stay in the safety of his vehicle. He locked the doors.

His headlights revealed no other vehicles or people around. No loud music. No beer bottles or cans. No sign of trouble other than the lights occasionally blinking on and off. Probably a short in the wiring of the old cottage. Satisfied with the explanation, he picked up his radio and let the dispatcher know he was leaving.

Putting his car in reverse, he looked in the rear-view mirror. He turned quickly in his seat. Behind him sat a scruffy-looking man dressed in a dirty, different-century shirt and a brimmed, black hat. He looked like something out of a swashbuckling movie, but Glen saw the lines of the backseat through him.

As if frozen by a sudden sub-zero wind, Glen sat frozen in place. The specter was transparent yet moving. A straggly beard and stringy hair surrounded the face that was there, yet not there.

The rough-looking apparition smiled, exposing a gold tooth shining in the lights of the dashboard.

Glen's hair stood on end as the ghostly figure said, "Goin' somewhere?"

In the blink of an eye and a cloud of sand and gravel, the officer made a U-turn with his cruiser. More gravel flew out from under the tires as the officer urged the vehicle to go faster. Only when he was back at the station would he feel safe again. His report of the incident would be yet another story added to the collection of strange occurrences at the crazy woman's house.

Chapter 2

Essie

Essie Bunny hurried down the long hallway of her underground home in Germany to reach the top of the long, winding stairs leading to the basement. Rushing down the steps, she finally came into the busy chocolate-egg factory. The Easter holiday was quickly approaching, and the factory was in full-production mode.

She searched the aisles along the conveyor belts that moved the forms that molded the liquid chocolate. Not seeing her husband, she moved to the next aisle where colored icings were being added to the newly formed chocolate eggs. Normally, she'd have taken the time to watch as the strings of colored frosting formed lace, ribbons, and flowers on the chocolate surfaces as they went by, but today, she didn't have the time.

Moving on to the aisle where crème eggs were being filled, she saw her husband, Easter Bunny, talking with a worker as the crew packaged the finished eggs. Essie yelled, but the noise of the factory floor drowned out her voice. She waved her arms, but the conversation was intense enough that no one looked her direction.

Trotting down the long aisle, she quickly closed the space between them. He turned to smile at her, but held up a hand to let her know to wait her turn. Her husband yelled above the din of the equipment, instructing the worker on where to put the eggs in the warehouse after they were packaged.

Essie bit her tongue to keep from yelling at Easter what she had to say was more important than boxing his eggs, but she knew he'd never agree with her. She turned away to keep from showing his worker her displeasure at having to wait. Her foot started to tap off the microseconds.

The urgency of her problem prodded her to set aside the last grain of patience. She spun around and glared. The eyes of the worker widened, causing Easter to turn around and look at her. With a final word of instruction, he took his wife by the arm and pulled her down the aisle toward his office.

Jerking her arm away from his firm grip, she walked beside him through the busy equipment to the small room in one corner of the factory. Shutting the door behind them, the noise of the factory was muted as Easter took his seat behind his neat desk. He rubbed his brow with the force of a man with too much to do in too little time.

"Honey, please, I've told you not to interrupt me while I'm with the workers." He folded his arms and leaned back in his chair, rocking it slightly as he stared at her. The lack of cartilage in his nose meant it hung down his face like the drip on the side of a candle, making his nostrils appear as slits.

Essie leaned over his desk. She was a grown woman and didn't need to be told the rules. She was the mother of thirteen and an enforcer of rules. Having rules thrown back at her gave her the equivalent of road rage. Gritting her teeth to hold back the burning words that threatened to cause a huge row with her husband, she managed to growl, "I know that. If it wasn't important, I wouldn't be here."

Picking up his Best Dad in the World coffee cup, he took a sip and wrinkled his limp nose at the taste. "Where's Sue, Jenny, and Ned?" he asked as he put the cup back on his desk and pushed it away.

The faces of the youngest of their thirteen children flashed through Essie's mind. After the phone call, she'd set them in front of the one-eyed babysitter and started their favorite movie. Although she felt sure the six-year-old triplets would still be there when she got back, a twinge of worry pricked her into hurried action.

"The kids are watching a movie with strict instructions to stay on the sofa until I get back." She stood up and crossed her arms. "I got a call from Florida. A call from the Sarasota Sheriff Department. About Mother's cottage. And it was not a pleasant call."

Easter quit rocking in his chair. "Trouble?"

Essie nodded.

Easter frowned. "Realtors again?"

Essie shook her head.

"Did someone break in the house?"

She shook her head again.

"Then what?" His fingers provided a drum roll while waiting for her to explain.

"Ghosts." Essie watched him as he froze in place for a few seconds before breaking out in raucous laughter. She crossed her arms in a huff. "It's not funny. The sheriff says the cottage is haunted. Says it has ghosts."

Easter covered his mouth to suppress his amusement. "Of course, it does! That's what Peg Leg and Rummy Jones are! Hannah left them there guarding the place for you. They're doing what you wanted them to. Keeping people away because it's haunted."

Clicking her tongue, Essie replied, "They've turned Mother's cottage into the most haunted place in Florida. Or that's the rumor that's going around according to the sheriff. The lights flash on and off all night long, and all kinds of ruckus goes on during the full moons. Paranormal people want to poke around the place and want to get inside to do whatever it is they do. The sheriff says to come check it out. Insists upon it."

She looked at him to see if he was listening. "I need to go to Florida."

Easter stared at her, shaking his head slightly. He rubbed his temples as he laughed lightly. "I guess I'm not surprised. Whoever heard of using ghosts as a security system. And pirate ghosts to boot. Not the most trustworthy type of guards."

Essie sank into a chair and half-heartedly joined her husband in his laughter. "Seems silly, but Hannah assured us it would work. No one would come around if they thought the cottage was haunted. If they did, her friends would scare them off. Who knew they'd attract attention to the cottage?"

"They're bored. That's why they're causing trouble."

Essie stared at her husband. The eyeroll that wanted to happen would raise the level of argument. She fought it off. "When did you become a ghost expert?"

"That's what our kids would do. How different could they be from kids?"

Easter's phone rang. He looked at it like he was going to ignore it, but with a moan of resignation, he picked it up, said his name, and listened. After a few seconds, he said, "I'll be there in a few minutes. Don't touch it until I get there." He hung up and turned back to Essie. "The forklift won't start."

Essie knew her time was limited before he ran off. "The sheriff said when they send deputies out to investigate, strange things happen. He's run out of deputies willing to go. People are calling him for permission to go in and exorcise the demons. Of course, he can't do that, but he suggested we check into it. From the tone of his voice, he sounded pretty fed up with the whole situation."

Easter sighed like a man who knew he wasn't going to influence her already-made decision. "So, you're going back to Florida. Can you wait a couple of weeks? Our egg delivery is coming up, and I need your help getting organized. You can go after that." He slapped the desk with his hand as he stood. "Better yet, it was Hannah's idea. Let her go check it out."

Essie let out a grunt as she stood to go. "We agreed to only go there together when we can visit Mother again. We'd planned to be there after Easter. It's only a couple of weeks early." Running her finger along the edge of the desk, she avoided his stare as her heart started beating faster as she summoned the nerve to say what she was thinking. "Santa and some of his elves might come help you. It's their off season. They're probably free."

"No elves!" Easter started pacing behind his desk. Running his fingers through his hair, he declared, "I don't want them prowling around here. When I gave them the tour in January, they were all over the machinery, trying to tweak it or suggesting how to make it run better. I got this place the way I like it, and I don't want it messed up."

Essie put her hands on her hips. "They gave you good suggestions. You should listen to them. Have an open mind about doing things better. Santa's your brother-in-law, and I'd think you'd at least respect his workers' opinions. Everyone else on the planet respects them. I don't know why you can't too."

Easter snorted, flopping his nose out. "Santa's nice enough, but those elves of his...it's like they're workaholics looking for a place to get down to business. You saw how they were all over my equipment, checking fluid levels, checking chains, and everything you can imagine. That's what I do! I don't need their help!"

He stopped long enough to take a breath which seemed to calm him down. "Although it would be nice to have a capable, steady crew. I envy his workforce stability." He looked off into space. His entrepreneurial wheels were obviously turning.

Glancing at her cell phone and noting the time, Essie grew more impatient. She knew her youngest three well enough to know they wouldn't be sitting quietly in front of the TV very long before looking for mischief. "I'll let you work that out with him another day. Right now, I need to go to Florida to see what's going on."

"Who will take care of the kids while you're gone? I certainly don't have time to—"

"I'll take care of that. We distribute chores. The older kids can watch the younger ones. I won't be gone long, no more than a week. It'll do them good." At least, she hoped it would.

"I have to go, Easter. You might as well accept that." Essie went toward the door.

Easter ran around the desk and stopped her before she could leave. "You know I support you in your decisions, but please reconsider. These coming two weeks is our most busy time. I need you." He looked at her with pleading eyes. "The children need you."

Essie closed her eyes to avoid the guilt-provoking stare of her husband. He was right. It was the worst time to leave. Sharon and Hannah could take care of the matter, but they had a pact. They'd agreed to go only when the three of them could be there together.

The moon was waning. Maybe Peg Leg and Rummy Jones would settle down for a while. Maybe she should ignore the sheriff's pleas and go in a couple of weeks. Peace between her and Easter would be preserved.

Opening her eyes, she was a little surprised to see Easter still standing there. His pleading eyes had been replaced with ones of sympathy. He took her hand as he said, "You can stay longer if you wait a couple of weeks. I'll be free to help watch the kids." He lifted her hand up to his lips.

The soft kiss on the back of her hand sent goosebumps up her arm. The sudden exit of enthusiasm left her feeling deflated. She couldn't argue with his logic. "Let me talk to Hannah and Sharon. We can arrange to go in a couple of weeks. I'll call the sheriff back and tell him to let it ride until then."

Easter gave her a quick peck on the cheek. "You won't regret it." He hurried out of his office and back to work, leaving Essie alone in his office.

Fearing her triplets were rearranging her neat home, she raced upstairs to the house. Her t-shirt was slightly damp from the workout getting up the steps. She was surprised to find them still mesmerized by the movie, still where she'd left them. Jenny had her long hair draped over the arm of the sofa, while Sue was leaning against the other end. Ned was sitting on the back of the sofa, leaning against the wall. Any place high and daring, that's where she always found him. Inwardly laughing, she decided to leave him where he was. She'd deal with his pleading to stay there after her phone call.

Sitting down at her long dining table where she could keep an ear on the activities in the living room, Essie dialed her sister Hannah Horseman's number. Loud background noises, like pans banging together, nearly drowned out Hannah's voice when she answered the phone.

Essie shouted, "Did I call at a bad time?"

Hannah laughed. "This is the perfect time. We're cleaning out the shed, and I need to rest for a few minutes."

Essie heard a muffled, "Keep working, boys" as the background noise volume diminished.

"Hang on while I call Sharon," she said.

Her sister Sharon Claus lived out in the frozen north. Provided no sunspots were interfering with her cell service, she was usually easy to call.

After several rings, Sharon answered. All three sisters were on the call. Essie relayed the Sarasota sheriff's messages about the lights, the moans during the full moons, his frantic request for help in dealing with whatever was going on in the cottage. "He wants us to check on the cottage. I think we should go. Something weird is going on."

"Why?" Hannah asked. "Rummy Jones and Peg Leg are doing what we asked them to. Tell him the cottage is haunted. That's all he needs to know."

"But...but..." Sharon's voice trembled. "We didn't ask them to disturb the neighbors. I thought if people came around, they'd scare them off. It sounds like they're attracting people to the cottage. We don't need anyone prowling around the grandfather clock." Her voice was high pitched and tense.

"Get a bag, Sharon," Hannah said with a tired voice. "There's no reason to get upset."

Essie switched the phone to the other ear. They didn't need one of Sharon's panic attacks again, especially over the phone where no one could do anything to help. This matter needed everyone's input to decide what to do. "Sharon, take a deep breath. Nothing's wrong that a visit to the cottage won't fix."

Hannah cleared her throat and a loud sigh came through. "I should have mentioned this earlier, but I knew something was going on. The electric bill has been higher the past couple of months. Now I know why. They're playing with the lights."

Essie rubbed her forehead to push the tension aside. She felt a tug on her blouse and looked down into the eyes of her triplets. The movie was over, and they were restless. Trouble would follow unless she distracted them.

Into the kitchen they went where she gave them cookies to eat. It's all she could do with one hand while holding the phone with the other. Watching the triplets skip away, she worried about where she'd find the crumbs later. No sense fretting about it now. Her sisters needed her attention.

Pacing in the kitchen, she continued. "If you could hear the strain in the sheriff's voice, you'd understand how frustrated he is. Plus—" she looked around to make sure no eavesdroppers were around before whispering, "—Mother's money is still hidden inside. And we've got to protect the clock. If it gets tipped over and broken, what would we do? We can't call Father or Mother without it. I think we should go see what's going on."

"Now?" Hannah said it in an almost screeching voice. "Your holiday is coming up quickly. Aren't you busy?"

Tapping her fingers on the countertop, Essie clenched her teeth. "Easter asked we wait for a couple of weeks."

"I bet he did," Hannah said, with an I'm-right tone. "We decided to go down later this summer. Let's stick to the plan."

Essie resisted the urge to let out a yell of frustration.

It would do no good and would likely make things worse. Holding the phone away from her, she took a giant breath and let it out slowly before speaking into the phone again. "What should I tell the sheriff to tell our neighbors? That we don't have time to come?"

Sharon let out a frantic, "No!"

One side of Essie's mouth went up in a smirk. Sharon was easy to persuade to do anything. Just appeal to her sense of compassion and consideration for others. Hannah, the obstinate sister, would be much harder to persuade.

Sharon's quick breathing came over the phone. The panic had started. Surely she had a paper bag handy. If she didn't get it under control, the phone call was a waste of time.

Sharon squeaked, "Our neighbors will hate us if we don't quiet things down soon." The sound of a crinkling paper bag came through the phone. "Essie and I could take care of it by ourselves," Sharon offered. "We promise not to call Mother until you get there, Hannah."

Hannah's impatient sigh was easily heard in the phone before she said, "Sharon dear, we're dealing with ghosts. You really want to handle them without me there?"

Cold adrenaline flowed through Essie's veins and made her hair stand on end. Ghosts were not her forte. That gift belonged to Hannah. Without Hannah's support, she'd not go to Florida. The neighbors could hate them all they wanted, but she wouldn't deal with ghosts without Hannah there.

Sharon took in a quick gasp. "Dumb idea. I won't go unless you go! I can't handle ghosts! Maybe I shouldn't go at all. You girls go take care of it. Let me know what you find out."

Still feeling the creepiness of ghosts, Essie agreed. "Hannah, go see about it."

Hannah spoke in a miffed tone. "Breaking our agreement, girls?"

Essie circled in the kitchen, wondering how to handle

this. This issue should be a simple one. Go talk to the ghosts guarding the house. Tell them to settle down. But with everything concerning the cottage, nothing was simple where three personal views were concerned.

Essie squeezed her eyes shut and rubbed them. The tension was building. They had to avoid falling back into their habit of bitterly arguing with each other. Tact. Like her mother had. That's what she needed. She needed to find it within her tumultuous self.

Right or wrong, a decision needed to be made. Being the oldest, it was her responsibility. At times like this, she wished she'd been the baby of the family.

"Our agreement is not negotiable. We all go, or no one goes. Hannah, can you possibly make a quick trip before summer? It shouldn't take but a day or two to convince them to hold it down or get out."

Another loud, impatient exhale came over the phone. "Give me a few minutes." Her muted but gruff mumbling expressed her displeasure at her sisters as she did whatever she was doing on the other end of the connection. After a moment, she said, "You're lucky. Looks like I can make it in a couple of weeks. We'll go see what Peg Leg and Rummy Jones are up to. And don't worry, I can deal with them."

Essie felt the tension and her body ease. Hannah's schedule meshed with hers which would please Easter. Now for the tricky question. "Sharon, can Santa take us in his sled? I hate to impose on him, but we'd get down there in the least amount of time for the least amount of money." She held her breath waiting for the answer.

"I don't know for sure," Sharon responded. "He likes to give the reindeer the spring months off so they can rest up from their global trip. I'll have to ask him."

"Could you do it now? We need to know whether to make plane reservations or not."

Another loud, impatient sigh came across the connection, but Essie couldn't tell who it came from. It didn't matter. No one was happy, but it wasn't her fault. They had to settle the arrangements and bicker about them later.

"Just a minute. I think I know where he is. Hang on."

While they waited for Sharon to find Santa, Essie and Hannah passed the time with small talk about their children. Hannah's two boys were busy with school activities. They were old enough to get involved with after-school soccer games and still have time to do their chores at home. Essie talked about her many children's activities at school and playing in sports. Both sisters had almost full-time bus-driver jobs getting their kids to after-school games and piano and guitar lessons. Motherhood was putting a lot of miles on their cars.

To their surprise, they heard Santa chime in on their conversation. "Enjoy these days. The children will be gone and on their own soon enough." He let out a lively, "Ho! Ho! Ho!" before getting to business. "I don't mind taking you down there. The new moon is on the fourteenth. We need to go that night, but how long are you staying? I cannot take the reindeer out if the moon is too bright. Not this time of year."

Essie hadn't thought of that, but Hannah let her off the hook. "One or two days should be enough time to get those ornery ghosts to behave. If not, I'll get Headless to come down. He can handle ghosts better than anyone I know."

A shudder tremored through Essie. Her brother-in-law Headless Horseman with his unattached head was nice enough. He had a handsome face. But there was no getting used to seeing him carrying it around under his arm.

Maybe he should go take care of the business for them. He wasn't part of their pact, so he could go alone. He could do to the ghosts whatever he needed to do to handle them. Exactly what that was, her ability wouldn't allow her to imagine it. Still, it wasn't his responsibility. It was theirs and theirs alone.

"It's settled then," she said, trying to clear her mind of the strange images flashing through it. "Santa, you'll pick us up on the fourteenth and we'll go to the cottage to see what's going on. Email me with the time and I'll be ready. You should be ready to be hugged a lot so count in a little time to say hello to the kids."

Santa let out a hardy cry. "Ho! Ho! Ho! I always make time for hugs. I'll get with NORAD and make the arrangements. See you ladies on the fourteenth!"

Essie hung up and sat on the sofa. The triplets were nowhere to be seen. The call must have taken longer than she thought. Quiet in the house was a sure sign they were into something they shouldn't be. Ghosts or triplets? Which was the greater threat? One she couldn't do anything about. The other, she could. Following the comfortable option, she hurried off to discover what mess she needed to clean up.

Chapter 3

Sharon

Two weeks after Essie's phone call, Sharon Claus finished packing her suitcase. Unlike her last visit to her mother's cottage, she had clothes suitable for the spring weather in Florida, thanks to the last shopping trip she'd made with her sisters. She zipped the suitcase closed but left it there for Santa to haul to the awaiting sled out front. She sat on the edge of the bed.

The dark sky outside her window danced with color. Sharon went to her rocking chair and watched the display. This was her comfortable place. Her panic attacks were few here. Taking care of Santa and the elves was her special happiness. It was what she was meant to do with her life. Why should she leave this serenity? Especially to go be around ghosts.

Sharon's heart shrank away from the thought. Its rapid flight from the terrible thought made her dizzy, and her breath came quickly. Her hand went to a nearby paper bag. She held its open mouth over her face. The bag wrinkled as it went in and out with her fast breathing. Slowly, the bag's wrinkling diminished, and her breathing was restored to a pre-panic pace.

She rocked in the chair in her happy place. The nights were getting shorter as spring approached. The window next to her looked out at the colorful sky dance that tinted the white landscape around her home. The changing colors comforted her as she faced the task ahead.

It was inevitable. She had two foes that needed conquering: fear itself and her fear of ghosts. Hannah wasn't afraid of them, and Essie probably wasn't either, but both were more courageous about everything. Surely they wouldn't let anything bad happen. Maybe there was nothing to fear. Ghosts were only the spirits of the dead walking around. Inside her mother's house.

Fear forced her body to shudder like an earthquake. The bag returned to her face to prevent more panic. There was only one thing to do. Put on a brave face and stay outside the cottage until Hannah handled the situation.

Santa sauntered into the bedroom, took one look at the suitcase on the bed, and sighed. He gingerly took the handle and gave a mighty heave. He stumbled backward as the suitcase flew into the air, which brought an outburst of surprise. "It's light! You didn't pack everything you own this time."

Sharon laughed as she rose from her rocking chair. "I have the right clothes this time. Florida attire doesn't weigh nearly as much as Arctic attire. The sleigh ready?"

Setting the suitcase down, Santa gave Sharon a sweet peck on the cheek. "All is ready for our trip. If it'll be any comfort to you, I'll stay at the cottage for a little bit. If you don't think you want to stay, I'll bring you home. You don't have to stay there."

"Thanks," Sharon whispered so she didn't get too choked up with his touching promise. His assurance to stay there for her helped her anxiety. She had an out. The trip didn't seem quite as bleak.

The two of them made their way out to the front room where the elves wished them a good journey. The elf children had colored pictures for her to take along so she'd remember them. Sharon planted a kiss on the tops of their heads. Martha, the elf who was her best friend, gave her sack lunches for the trip and a supply of paper bags to use during her panic attacks. Sharon smothered her in a bear hug.

Putting a heavy coat over her pink blouse and black slacks, she stepped out into the cold. In front of their stone house in the middle of the snowy plain of the North Pole sat Santa's nearly empty sleigh with eight small reindeer in front, stomping their feet and tugging on the harnesses. Elwin the elf sat in the front of the sleigh, holding the reindeer back as best he could. The young ones were especially hard to control.

Santa rushed to the sled, threw the suitcase in the back, and took over the reins. Sharon followed him out and climbed into the back of the sled. There, a red wooly blanket awaited her. She curled up under it and felt the sleigh take off. Peeking out, she saw the sun's faint light on the southwestern side of the horizon. The sky to the north was filled with innumerable stars. The colorful lights of the aurora played.

The farther south they went, her dread grew stronger. Unable to overcome her mounting anxieties, she snuggled down under the blanket for a cat nap.

A nudge on her foot awoke Sharon. "We're near Essie's house," Elwin said. "Want to watch as we come in for a landing?"

Sharon sat up and rubbed her eyes. Only a few faint lights below gave any indication they were over civilization. Easter and Essie Bunny lived far out in the country to keep their factory hidden from prying eyes. Their children attended the small schools nearby, but no one knew Easter delivered candy eggs around the world. Or if they'd heard such rumors, they dismissed them as folklore.

Santa circled the Bunny house and guided the reindeer down. They landed softly on the grass outside the front gate. As soon as they skidded to a stop, the front door opened, and a mob of people poured out of the house, rushing toward the sled. Elwin jumped out to calm the reindeer while Santa ran to meet the crowd.

Holding his finger over his lips, he shushed them. "You must be quiet!" he said to the children who wanted to pet the reindeer. "These are our trainees and aren't used to the crowds. Please go slow and stay calm." He led the children over where he helped them around the reindeer who snorted and pawed the ground. Elwin's expert touch kept them calm. The children approached the reindeer slowly and patted them gently, giving them treats of apples and carrots.

Sharon yawned and got out of the sled. Essie and Easter were coming toward her, arm in arm like newlyweds. Seeing how in love they were after 20 years and 13 children made her smile. Her nieces and nephews were blessed to have a loving set of parents. She opened her arms to invite her sister into her embrace.

Essie spoke first as she hugged Sharon. "You ready for this?" She let out a skeptical laugh. "I know I'm not."

Sharon shook her head as Santa put Essie's bag in the sled. "I don't want to go, but I'm sticking to our agreement. We go together. But thinking about it makes me a nervous wreck!"

The looming panic attack faded when several of the children came up to give their Aunt Sharon a hug. "My goodness," she said to them, "shouldn't you be in bed? It's almost midnight!"

Sadie jumped around her, not able to hold in her excitement. "Mom said we could stay up to see you and Uncle Santa. Can we sit in the sleigh?"

Sharon laughed. "Of course! But watch out for our luggage." She helped Sadie, Sue, Alan, and Jenny into the sleigh. They marveled over the soft, warm blanket that would keep their mother and aunt warm on their journey.

"Quickly, children," Easter said as he watched the activities, "tell your mother good-bye. They have a long way to go before morning."

The children gathered around Essie, and she spent a moment with each one, giving them last minute instructions, telling them no fighting was allowed, reminding them of their responsibilities while she was gone, and giving them each a hug and a kiss.

Santa spoke with Easter as he watched the hubbub. As Easter gathered his children, Santa went to help Elwin adjust harnesses and pet the reindeer. Santa climbed in the sleigh, with Elwin close behind him.

Essie and Sharon climbed aboard the sleigh and covered up with the warm blanket. With a last wave and the ringing of children's voices in the air, the sleigh took off into the dark, spring night.

Chapter 4

Hannah

In the woods of Pennsylvania, Hannah Horseman sat on the front porch of her farmhouse with her husband, Headless. The stars shone bright in the moonless sky. Near the barn, one of their horses nickered.

Headless and Hannah sat on the porch swing, gently rocking back and forth. His head sat on the wide porch rail while the rest of him sat beside Hannah. Her arms were wrapped around his muscular arm, and his hand was on her knee.

"I checked the boys before I came out," she said as she lay her head against his shoulder. From there, she saw his loving eyes staring at her, starlight reflecting in his dark eyes. "They're handsome and peaceful when they sleep."

Headless whispered, "They miss you when you're gone."

"Do they miss me, or do they want me back so Mrs. Hagg will leave?" Hannah and Headless laughed together, then shushed each other so they wouldn't wake the boys.

"A little of both," Headless said softly. "Even I get a little creeped out when she's around. She's a nice lady, but she slinks around so quietly I can't keep track of her. I turn around, and there she is. It scares me so bad I jump. She's made me drop my head a time or two, and I don't like that."

"We could get her to wear a bell around her neck."

She watched a sly grin spread across his face above

the rail as his body shook with a quiet laugh. "Like a black cat. But that wouldn't be kind. Don't get me wrong. She's nice enough, but the boys are afraid of her because she's curled and bent, like a jack-o-lantern left out too long. Smells that way too."

Hannah gave Headless a gentle rap on the knuckles. "What an awful thing to say about our best neighbor! She's been very kind to us. A true friend who keeps our secret. We shouldn't be talking about her that way."

Headless agreed. He asked the elephant-in-the-room question hanging over them. "Have you decided what you're going to say to Rummy Jones and Peg Leg when you get there?"

Hannah sat up straight, rubbed her forehead, and searched her thoughts on a solution to the problem. Many things twirled in her head from their other discussions about it. No idea would stay still long enough for her to grab on to. Only the weakest straws lingered long enough for consideration. "Tell them to stop it, I guess. I'm surprised they're causing trouble. They're usually mellow guys and better behaved, even though they're pirates."

"I've known them since they were alive, and they never caused any problems before. There must be something else going on. Maybe we should leave the boys with Mrs. Hagg so I can come with you. I'm better at dealing with ghosts than you are."

Her heart ached to say yes to him, but her brain filled with reasons why he shouldn't. "The boys would hate it. She can't help with chores in the barn because she scares the horses. As much as I hate to say it, one of us should be here to see after the chores and keep the boys calm with her around."

With a sad look on his face, Headless sighed his surrender. "You're right as usual. Our mares will be foaling soon, and it's important for me to be here for that."

In the distance, a dog barked. The horse in the corral nickered again as it pawed the ground. A soft night breeze drifted across the porch. Hannah leaned back against his shoulder again, taking comfort in the heat of his body. She held out her feet with her sequined shoes. They sparkled in the faint starlight.

"I'll tell Rummy Jones and Peg Leg they can either do what I say, or I'll send you down to deal with them. That might put the fear in them."

Headless scowled from the porch railing as he clenched his fists in the swing. "You tell them if I have to come down there to take care of this, I'll be bringing our hellhounds with me. I haven't turned them loose on anyone lately, and they'd love nothing better than to maul two unruly ghosts."

He gave a shrill whistle. "Here, Shuck! Here, Styx!" In a short moment, two large black hounds with glowing red eyes came out of the darkness and bounded up the front steps. Dancing around the feet of their master, they nosed around until Headless pulled a snack for each from his pocket. In a quick, slobbery fashion, they swallowed their treats. They moved to Hannah to see what she had. She scratched them behind their ears and gave them back rubs. Shuck made his way to the side of Headless and sat. Styx lay across Hannah's feet, let out a sigh, and closed her red eyes.

Hannah giggled a little. "I won't tell them they're our family pets."

Reaching out to pet the head of his furry companion, Headless told her, "Don't be fooled. They can tear anything limb from limb if I told them to. Including ghosts."

The hounds jumped to their feet, staring out into the night sky. An unexpected breeze came up suddenly, brushing against their faces. Hannah looked up in time to see the Christmas sleigh circling the yard. The horses neighed from the pasture, and their hoofbeats sounded from the corral. Headless grabbed his head and put it on the cradle sitting atop his shoulders.

Hannah checked her cell phone for the time. One thing about Santa, he kept a tight schedule, but then again, he had to be back home before sunup. She looked back toward the house. She wanted to peek in on the boys again before she left. They may miss her, but she missed them more. Just one more look…

The sound of tiny feet landing on the lawn in front of her house told her time was up. She gave Headless a quick kiss before their privacy was completely gone. He picked up her luggage and followed her down the porch steps.

A squeal of delight sounded from the sleigh as Sharon got out, followed closely by Essie. Hannah received a bear hug around her waist from her shorter, middle sister. Her taller, older sister hugged her shoulders. Unable to resist, she hugged them back as tightly as she could. A year ago, the moment wouldn't have been possible. A year ago, she despised her sisters. Thanks to her mother's devious planning, they were reunited and back on the sisterhood track.

As they pulled apart, Essie told Hannah, "I see you still have your sequined shoes." Essie held out her foot to show her own twinkling shoes in the dim starlight.

Sharon held out her foot to show her footwear matched her sisters' shoes. Silly giggles sounded across the yard.

The sisters turned to greet Headless as he put Hannah's suitcase in the sleigh where Santa stashed it in the back with the other luggage. Hopping down, Santa stuck his hand out to his brother-in-law. "Good to see you, Headless! How have you been?" Santa shook his hand vigorously.

So vigorously that the handshaking made the loose head start to wobble in its cradle. Headless put up his free hand to steady it on its perch. "I'm doing well as long as I don't lose my head." He pulled his hand back from Santa and adjusted his head so that it was firmly in the cradle. "You think these ladies are prepared to deal with what awaits them at the cottage?"

"I think we're married to tough women who can handle anything."

Sharon came up beside Santa and took his arm. "I think Essie and Hannah can handle it just fine."

Santa patted her hand. "You'll do fine. Be brave, my darling. Show those nasty ghosts who's boss."

"He's right," Headless added as he put his arm around Hannah. "You have nothing to fear. Be tough with them. They can't hurt you. Besides, I told Hannah I'd come down there to handle things if I need to. If I come, they'll wish they'd listened to you."

"See," Santa said to Sharon, "there's a backup plan. Everything will turn out all right." Santa let out a hardy "Ho! Ho! Ho!" as he motioned for his passengers to climb aboard.

As Hannah was getting into the sleigh, the front door flung open and Huntley and Horace came racing out. "We want to go too!" they shouted as they tried to climb aboard beside their mother.

Headless took each one by the arm and pulled them back. "You're staying here with me," he said gruffly. "This trip is for your mother and her sisters. We'll go next time." He turned them toward the house and gave them a gentle nudge.

Just out of reach of his father, Huntley turned around, his angry expression carried into his voice's tone. "Mother always goes without us, and Mrs. Hagg comes over here. I hate her! She's ugly! And she stinks! I can't stand to look at her! It's no fair!" He screamed out the last three words. They hung in the air for a moment like a puff of smoke before dissipating.

Hannah was away from the sleigh like a shot, passing Headless as he started toward their son. Hannah grabbed Huntley by the front of his t-shirt and pulled him up close to her. "I won't allow you to speak so cruelly about my friend. If I ever hear of you saying such horrible things about her again, you'll be grounded until you turn 30." She pulled him closer to her face as she added through clenched teeth, "You understand me? I mean what I say."

Huntley cowered in fear at the ferocity of his

mother's wrath.

Horace came up beside his brother, eyes wide with surprise and fear, and hung on to Huntley. They nodded in obedience.

"I'm sorry, Mother." Huntley's voice and chin quivered as tears formed in his eyes. "I won't do it again."

"You better not! And for saying it the first time, you will do dishes every night while I'm gone. Hear that, Headless?"

Headless came up beside her and pulled a frightened Huntley away from her. He smoothed out the front of his t-shirt. "You don't mind doing the dishes, do you, Huntley?"

"No sir, not at all."

"Good boy. Why don't you go say bye to your aunts and uncle while I speak with your mother. Horace, you too." Horace gave Hannah a wide berth before running to the sleigh.

Headless put his arm around Hannah and pulled her away from the others. She already knew what he was going to say and didn't want to hear him say it. "I know. I know. I overreacted."

"By a whole lot," he said gently. "But so did he. He may be a teenager, but he's a boy who misses his mother when she's gone. Forgive him for disguising it as he did. Poor Mrs. Hagg is the innocent bystander in his internal drama."

Hannah covered her face with her hands. Her flash of anger was guilt. Guilt over leaving them. Guilt over making them stay with Mrs. Hagg. She knew they didn't like her because she smelled funny and was spooky. But if they could see past that, that her beautiful inside was hidden beneath the ugly outside, they'd see her differently.

Now Huntley was probably glad she was leaving after she treated him horribly. She was his mother and supposed to love him. Tears threatened her makeup, and she blinked hard to hold them back. Pinching the bridge of her nose tightly helped a little.

"Mom?"

Huntley's contrite voice sounded sweet to her ears. She spun around to see her 15-year-old son standing there.

"Mom, I'm sorry. It's okay if Mrs. Hagg comes over. She makes good stew. I know you have to go, but I'm going to miss you."

Hannah reached out to her son and smothered him in an embrace. "And I'm sorry for yelling at you. I feel horrible about it." She whispered in his ear, "I don't want to go, but I have to. Did you know your aunts are terrified of ghosts? They won't be able to do this without me." She let him go and watched his dark eyes staring at her. She wondered when he'd grown as tall as her.

Huntley cocked his head. "Afraid of ghosts? Why? We have lots of friends who are ghosts. Are they ghost non-believers?"

A smile came to Hannah's face unbidden. "Not at all. It's just they haven't been around them like we have. They get frightened. Once they know them better, they'll understand them and will stop being scared."

She ran her hands through his bed-mussed hair. "We told you about Peg Leg and Rummy Jones causing problems. We have to protect the cottage and the magic clock. If they don't cooperate, your dad will come take care of them. Please be good for Mrs. Hagg, and I'll be back as quickly as I can. And I promise next time, we'll all go. And after that, just our family will go. Won't that be fun?"

Huntley smiled at her and hugged her tightly. Horace came up and hugged them. Hannah felt Headless encircle his family with his long arms and hug tightly. The boys protested they were being smothered. Laughing, the family pulled apart, and Hannah made her way to the sleigh.

When the sleigh touched down in front of the cottage in Florida, Hannah was the first to step out of the sleigh. Everything seemed fine. The whitewashed cottage on a small rise near the shore was quiet and dark, like it was supposed to be. In the distance behind it, rows of lights indicated where development encircled the stone cottage. How could sounds from the cottage travel that far above the sound of the ocean lapping at the sands of the beach?

As Santa unloaded their luggage, Hannah walked over to him. "I'd forgotten how fast this sleigh travels! We left my house only minutes ago. No wonder you can travel the world in one night! How do you do it?"

"Ho! Ho! Ho! It's part of the magic of Christmas! You believe, don't you?

"More than ever!" Hannah's attention was drawn away by the lights in the cottage flashing on and off.

An unearthly moan came from the house, sounding as if the structure was in great pain. The eerie silence that followed sent Essie to cower behind Hannah and Sharon to crouch behind Essie. Santa stood frozen in place, his eyes wide with questioning fear.

Slowly, another higher-pitched moan emitted from the house, growing in volume until it was heard above the sound of the surf before it stopped. Letting out a squeal of fright, Sharon jumped back into the sleigh. The sound of a paper bag crinkling in and out filled the air.

Rolling her eyes, Hannah started toward the porch. Whether Rummy Jones or Peg Leg was singing out, she didn't care. If her hound Styx was here, she'd send the dog in to drag those two rascals out of the cottage. She should have brought Styx with her. Her pet would have sent them on their way in short order, but it was too late to worry about that now.

She paused on the top step and turned around. Sharon was nowhere to be seen, but the large lump under the wool blanket was likely her. Essie stood behind Santa who had his hand on the sleigh, positioned to jump in. Elwin had a tight hold on the front reindeer that stomped and seemed ready to take off. He spoke softly to them, trying to calm them.

No sense going in without them. Unless they posed as a united front, the cantankerous ghosts might not leave. But she couldn't drag shivering cowards here to face them. Not only did she need to take the lead, she had to somehow instill courage in her spineless sisters. But how? She'd start with kind, encouraging words and move on from there.

Back down the steps she went and across the yard to the sleigh. "Come on, you two. We need to get down to business. There's nothing to be afraid of. They won't hurt you."

She watched for any sign of backbone. Nothing.

"If we run them out of here tonight, we can go home."

Still nothing.

"Our families would hardly know we'd left."

No one made a move.

"Cowards," she whispered to herself. Only one other thing she could try. Guilt. It was her greatest ally. She had to find a way to guilt them into facing their fears.

"What about the clock? We can't call Mother or Father for help if we can't get in the house."

The red, wool blanket moved. Essie blinked and hung her head.

Now to finish that off. "The cottage is ours. Let's retake it!"

Hannah pulled the blanket off Sharon and offered her hand to help her out of the sleigh.

Hannah smiled. Guilt always worked. "I won't let anything happen to you. Trust me. We can do this."

Sharon's eyes went between Santa and Hannah's offered hand. With a resigned sigh, she reached for Hannah's hand and pulled herself out. Santa helped her the last part of the way. She straightened her pink blouse and said, "You're right. Nothing is more important than the clock. I won't let anything stand between me and seeing Mother again."

Santa reached out to grab Essie as she tottered a little. She brushed him away and stood straighter. "If you promise nothing bad will happen, I'm behind you. Way behind you, but behind you nonetheless." She motioned for Hannah to lead the way.

Santa grabbed Sharon's arm. "Are you sure you want to stay? I need to get back home before sunrise, but I don't want to leave you if it's too much for you."

Sharon rushed into his arms and buried her face in his furry, red coat.

Hannah looked down at her feet so her sisters wouldn't see her face. If Sharon left, Essie likely would too. The whole affair was falling on her shoulders alone. Might as well. It was her husband's idea to use the ghosts for home security. It was up to her to make things right again. Headless said he'd come with the hounds to take care of them, but she'd rejected the idea. It was her mother's house, and it was up to the three sisters to take care of it, a noble sentiment she regretted now that she was here with her scaredy-cat sisters. But too late for that. She'd do it alone.

She was about to tell Sharon and Essie to go back when she heard the improbable.

"I'll stay. My sisters will take care of me."

Stunned by what she heard, Hannah watched Santa and Sharon give each other a long kiss. Santa climbed into the sleigh and motioned for Elwin to join him. Sharon linked arms with Essie and made her way toward the cottage.

Hannah couldn't seem to get her feet to move. What just happened? Sharon was turning down a ride back home? That didn't make sense.

Santa yelled at her and brought her out of her stupor.

"Be a good girl and take care of them. I can come back tomorrow night to get her or whoever wants to go home."

Not knowing whether to be happy her sisters were staying or to be mad at being called a girl, she nodded and waved before joining her sisters in their march to face the paranormal. She heard a whoosh as Santa and Elwin headed home, followed by a whimper from Sharon. Kitten-hearted Sharon. She wouldn't be much help, but Essie would stick with her. She had more backbone than...

The lights flicked on and off again, raising her ire.

Electricity cost money, and those two pirate ghosts had better be ready to pay for their play. She paused on her way up the steps and pulled her cell phone out of her pocket. If Santa came back tomorrow night, he could bring Headless and the hellhounds down. They'd get the pranksters out of there so fast they'd turn pale.

Still, if she did this herself, she'd show her sisters they didn't need to be afraid. Facing their fears would make them stronger. Time to take control and set the example.

Hannah stomped up the front porch steps. Another flash of light and a shriek came out of the cottage. Behind her, her sisters let out a shriek echoing the same high note.

Hannah stopped in front of the door of the cottage. Hot with rage, she shoved her phone back in her pocket. Enough was enough. Peg Leg and Rummy Jones were having a party. It was time to shut it down. She should have known better than to ask two pirates to help with anything. Why she let Headless talk her into it, she'd never know.

She quickly unlocked the door and flung it back in time to see a living room crowded with pirates, most of whom she didn't recognize. In an instance, they all disappeared.

Silence fell over the once-neat living room. Their mother's overstuffed leather sofa had been moved, and the overstuffed chair was turned over. Trash littered most of the horizontal surfaces. While shocked at the sight, Hannah let out a sigh of relief upon seeing the grandfather clock still sitting in its place, still showing the time to be nine-fifteen.

Essie stepped tentatively inside the door. "What a mess!" Essie cried out. "Those pirates are pigs!" She bent to pick up a pillow, then hugged it against her stomach as she continued to look around.

"What's happened to Mother's home?" Sharon cried out from behind Hannah. She leaned around the door frame to look in, but apparently wasn't brave enough to step inside. "They've trashed the place! It will take us forever to get it back to the way it was!"

Hannah shut the door behind them. Her face was hot. Her fists were so tight her nails dug into her palms. She bellowed, "I want to see Peg Leg and Rummy Jones right now!" She gestured at the floor in front of her. "If I don't see you two in the next few seconds, I will be calling Headless to come with our hellhounds!" The air moved around the room in a strange way.

Someone stood right behind Hannah, her hands clinging to the back of her blouse. Without looking to see which of her sisters was crowding her personal space, she put her hands on her hips. Staring into the empty space, she felt the presence of her two ex-friends.

Peg Leg's disembodied voice came from in front of Hannah. "This not be our fault."

"Yeah," Rummy Jones said out of the air, "they just showed up. We didn't ask them to come."

Hannah thundered, "I said show yourselves!" Her foot tapped while she waited for a response.

The pirate ghosts came into view, their hats in their hands.

"How did those shipmates of yours happen to get here? And how is it not your fault?"

Rummy Jones dug the toe of his boot into the floor. "They ain't exactly me shipmates…"

"It's Captain Fremont," Peg Leg said as he put his hat back on.

Hannah looked at her sisters. They shrugged. "Fremont? Never heard of him."

Rummy Jones looked around and whispered, "Scourge of the sea! He be a mean one."

Peg Leg elbowed his friend and gave him a harsh look. "You can't argue with him. He barged in and said he was supposed to meet his woman here."

"That be the truth, ma'am," Rummy Jones said, looking down like a thief standing before a judge.

Hannah crossed her arms. They seemed to be very nervous, with their fidgeting and cowering while they talked.

They seemed genuinely afraid of this Captain Fremont. "Meet his woman? Here? Why here?"

Rummy Jones held his arms out as he shrugged. "Twouldn't say." He backed away a little and put his hat on. "He's here ifn you want to talk with him."

Peg Leg nodded and caught Rummy Jones before he backed too far away. "We'll help you pick up the place. Come on, Rummy." He glided over and picked up a tissue lying on top of the upended overstuffed chair. Rummy Jones pushed a small stack of video cassettes with his foot until they were heaped under the lamp table.

Hannah continued tapping her foot as the two ghosts made feeble attempts to straighten the mess up. "I don't care about this captain or his woman. Essie got a call from the sheriff about all the noise you've been making. You've got people in these parts stirred up. That's not acceptable. I want you two, this Captain Fremont, and your other friends out of here before sunup!"

Rummy Jones picked up a throw pillow that had been treated according to its description. "Please, ma'am, don't send us away."

Peg Leg said as he took off his hat again, "We got no place to go. This be home to us now. We wanna stay. Please?"

The sound of several disembodied voices came from the hallway, pleading to stay as well. A shadow figure appeared in the corner beside the clock.

Essie stiffened and squeaked out, "You heard my sister! Get out of here!" She gingerly stepped around Hannah and stood taller, but not to her full height. "This is our mother's house, and we are taking it back."

Hannah felt Essie's trembling. She reached out and took her hand as she said, "We appreciate you watching over the place while we were gone, but your job is done. I'm asking nicely, please leave. You and your friends. You'll have to find another party place. There're other more deserted places to haunt."

No response came from the ghosts that were visible, and no sound came from those invisible in the hallway.

The sound of a paper bag being crumpled in and out filled the silence. Hannah turned to see Sharon peeking out from behind Essie with the bag over her mouth.

Rummy Jones looked from Hannah to the still silent captain by the clock and back again. "Ya can't mean it," said Rummy Jones with a tilted head and a quizzical look. "Ya asked us 'ere. We done what ye asked. Nobody hurt yer house. We kept our agreement. Ya don't mind us staying on, do ya? If we keep the noise down?"

Hannah watched as her timid sister's fearful eyes changed into little fireballs.

Sharon stepped out from behind Essie and lowered the paper bag. "Get out!" she roared with unexpected fury. "This is our mother's home, and we don't want you anywhere near here. Go!" Although she stood like a grizzly about to charge, Hannah noticed her slacks quivering.

Hannah smiled at her sisters. They'd finally found their courage and strength.

Chapter 5

Essie

Hearing Sharon's resolve against the ghosts gave Essie renewed strength. If Sharon could do it, so could she.

Hannah's fearlessness was amazing. And inspiring. Talking to ghosts wasn't comfortable or something she'd ever wanted to do. The urge to go home almost won the battle over the need to stay, but leaving meant never coming back again, and that wasn't an option. Her trembling eased as a flash of rage pushed the fright aside. This was her mother's house. They were taking it back. Like Sharon said.

Out of the corner of her eye, Hannah saw a movement by the grandfather clock. She tried not to look, knowing if she saw an apparition, it might lessen her resolve. She looked at Hannah instead. She didn't seem afraid of the ghosts. Acting like her would bring the elusive courage needed for this situation.

Three ghosts became visible as they came into the living room from the hallway. An unearthly stranger stood in front of the others. He wore a faded blue coat over his gray shirt and black pants. His high-top boots made the faint sound of footsteps as he walked closer to Hannah and Essie. A large-brimmed hat shaded his face.

From a place beside the clock, another ghost motioned the others to stop. His bicorn hat, double-breasted captain's coat, and demeanor signaled he was in charge. He moved and stopped in front of Hannah. "I like it here. We're staying. You abandoned the house. We claim it."

Fear pushed Essie back, but Hannah stood her ground. "And who might you be?"

The ghost took another step forward, getting in Hannah's face as he spoke. "They call me Captain Fremont. Captain Horatio Fremont."

He spread his feet and put his hands on his hips in a way that reminded Essie of Superman, only this guy was the antithesis of truth and justice. Essie looked at the four other ghosts standing behind him. Dressed like they were part of an old Hollywood swashbuckling movie, they hung back from the captain as their roles required.

The captain waved his hand toward the others, but not toward Rummy Jones and Peg Leg. "These are my men. We've commandeered your house. We need it while I wait for my woman."

Essie felt her cheeks burn. Commandeered? That must be pirate talk meaning taken over. He was declaring war for the cottage. They had to find the kryptonite to take this guy down. If they got rid of him, the others would follow.

She was no fighter. There had to be another way. Maybe they could bribe him to leave. Pirates liked loot, but where would ghosts use it? There had to be something else. Maybe if she were nice to him, he'd understand. Use the proverbial honey to lure flies out of the cottage.

She cleared her throat, hoping it would sound more authoritarian. "Captain Fremont," Essie said with as much authority as she could muster, "this house was not deserted. We—" she waved her hands toward her sisters, "—intend to live here when we can. We have the deed to the property, so we can prove it's ours in a court of law. I'm sure there's lighthouses or abandoned buildings somewhere you may inhabit while you wait for whoever you're expecting."

Captain Fremont let out a cynical laugh Essie was sure carried through the walls and out into the night. Honey may not work every time. Or this is no fly. He was a spider that needed a whap with a flyswatter. Or a shoe.

Hannah matched his laugh with one of her own. "The house is our territory. You're uninvited squatters. Get out now, or I'll have no choice but to call my husband, Headless Horseman. Ever heard of him?"

Captain Fremont narrowed his eyes. "Aye, I've heard of him." He pointed at the sisters. "We're not invaders. We're guests. We were invited here by Peg Leg Brown. Right, Peg? We're not leaving until Peg Leg asks us to." He walked over and put his arm around the cowering pirate, gripping him in a chokehold.

Essie observed the wide eyes and cringing form of Peg Leg as he stuttered a hesitant agreement. He was scared to death of Captain Fremont. But how could a ghost be scared to death? He was already dead.

"Enough of this nonsense!" Hannah said as she pulled her cell phone out of her pocket. "I'm calling Headless. He will bring his hellhounds here and force you to leave." She pushed a button and held the phone to her ears. The three other ghosts took a few steps back.

Captain Fremont leaned his head back and laughed. He glanced over his shoulder at his men huddled together. "Hellhounds don't scare me, but they do scare my crew. Let's parlay. Turn off your talking box."

Hannah held her phone to her ear for a few more seconds, then brought it down slowly and terminated the call. "Parlay? About what? You will leave our house. End of negotiation."

Captain Fremont signaled with his hand, and his crew set the overstuffed chair upright. The sword at his side stuck into the chair's leather but didn't puncture it. He took a seat and put his booted feet on the coffee table.

The action made Essie cringe on the inside. Her mother would not have approved.

"There's always something to negotiate." The captain removed his hat and put it on the arm of the chair. "Peg Leg tells me you asked him here to ward off intruders. We've done what you asked. No one has come around, except for the constables. They keep poking around here, but we run them off in short order."

"Stop doing that!" Essie cried out, surprised at hearing her voice sounding so harsh. "I've been getting phone calls about you scaring off his deputies. They come here to help us."

The captain gave her an icy stare, making her blood turn to ice. He continued to stare as if daring her to speak another word. Taking a step back, she wished someone would say something to take his attention away from her.

Hannah made a hand signal, and the pirates rushed to move the sofa back to its normal position. With a few grunts and groans, it was back to where it should have been.

Sharon and Essie took a few steps toward the open door, uncaring on whether Hannah came with them.

Instead of retreating, Hannah sat on the sofa end nearest her opponent and leaned forward, unafraid of the scalawag captain. "Peg Leg and Rummy Jones aren't going to be here forever, are you, boys."

The two pirates shook their heads vigorously and muttered, "No, ma'am."

With his hat in hand, Peg Leg said, "Captain, sir, me and Rummy told Mr. Horseman we'd leave when he told us to. We be men of our word. If Miz Hannah wants us to leave, we must go."

The sisters nodded their heads and individually offered their thanks.

Stroking his long gray beard, Captain Fremont gave a half grin. "They ain't part of my crew. They're free to leave. As for me and me crew," he pointed a thumb over his shoulder at the three unfamiliar specters, "we ain't going nowhere until my woman and our ship comes for us." He set his jaw and his mind.

"Your ship?" Hannah asked. "What's that got to do with our cottage?"

A faraway look filled the ghost's eyes as he continued to stroke his beard. "The Merribelle," he said in a wistful voice. "My beautiful ship carried me across the waves to any place I steered her. She be coming for me as soon as my woman gets here. During a full moon."

Counting on her fingers, Essie figured five full moons had passed since they returned home after their first visit. "During which full moon is it coming? There's one every month."

The captain shot up out the chair. He paced quickly in front of his crew, in front of the clock. With hands behind his back, he mumbled to himself. His crew cowered farther into the corner by the clock. The captain stopped, stretched out his arms, and let out a roar. Essie and Sharon clung to each other, but paused before going outside.

Something in the roar held Essie back. It was terrorizing, yet mournful. A roar meant to express heart pain rather than rage. There was more to this story, and she wanted to know it. She pried Sharon's hands from her arm and rubbed where the circulation had been cut off.

Drawing strength from Hannah, Essie crept to the dining table and drug two chairs behind her. Setting them near the door where she could easily escape if need be, she sat down while motioning for Sharon to join her. Sharon gingerly sat on the edge of the chair beside her, ready to spring to safety.

Hannah sat calmly on the sofa, tapping her fingertips together. She spoke softly, "What's going on, Captain Fremont? Who's this woman who was supposed to meet you?"

The ghost resumed his pacing with his hands clasped behind his back, his boots sounding soft steps on the hardwood floor. "A sad story it is. I was supposed to meet my true love after my last voyage and sail away. Only she wasn't there, and I can't find her."

"What do you mean you can't find her?" Essie asked, also in a whisper. "Where did you lose her?

A softer roar was uttered by the captain, soulful and sad. "She wasn't there," he whispered back. "She wasn't waiting for me like she promised to be." He wiped away something on his cheek.

A soft moan and a solitary sniff came from the huddled mob in the corner.

Essie's heart felt funny. Pirates didn't cry, did they? Nothing about their tears fit her preconceived notions about pirates. Weren't they heartless, murderous, thieving, lawless, loveless scoundrels?

Words drifted out of her memories. Something Easter had told her when they first met. Rejected love could hurt even the most stoic, the most strong, the most unlikely. The pirate in front of her was hurting like any spurned lover would be.

Enrapt with the story, she whispered, "Tell us about her."

The captain stopped in front of the silent clock. He looked at it, but never touched it. "Her name was Adella McPhee. She was beautiful, with long, dark hair and dark eyes and a feisty spirit who was a pleasure to duel with. By all that is sacred, she loved me, and I loved her. Our love was unbreakable and never-ending. Like nothing anyone ever felt before. We were one in soul. I was going to give up the sea, and we would be married. I would have done anything for her."

Another sniff came from the corner where his crew stood. One of them took off his cloth hat and dabbed his eyes.

Something pinched Essie's heart a little, forcing her eyes to moisten a little too much. "What happened?" she whispered.

The captain started pacing, his footfalls counting off his steps. "I was the best captain in the merchant navy. Never lost a fight. I was ruler of the sea. But my admiral thought he owned me. Treated me like I was his lackey. He was a fool. I was my own man. I owed him nothing. When I told him I was resigning from my post, he said, 'No, I'll never let ya go.' I nearly killed him that day. Many a day since, I wish I had.

"Aye," one of the crew yelled. "Ya should have killed him."

The captain paused long enough to cast a look at the crewman who shrunk back. Pacing again, he picked up the tale. "The admiral had chests full of gold in South America he wanted brought back to him. He'd trade my freedom and my silence for his gold. If I refused to follow his orders, he'd hang me for dereliction of duty. What else could I have done? I didn't want to leave her, but I didn't want a price on my head when we started our life together. I made that last voyage, even though I didn't want to. Me and my crew went there, we trekked through the jungle for days. Several good men died on that expedition. A year and a month after we left, we sailed into the harbor with his gold. He took possession of it and bought a fleet of ships for smuggling."

He took a rag out of his coat pocket and wiped his face. "Before I left to get his gold, my Adella promised me she'd wait for me at the White House Inn. I trusted her. She was a woman of her word so I trusted her."

A sniff and whimper came from the three ghosts. One wiped his nose on his tattered sleeve.

"I went to the inn, but she wasn't there. The innkeeper said she'd never come. I looked everywhere for her. I asked everyone if they'd seen her. At last, in the back of an old pub, a drunk man told me he'd heard she'd married another man. They left the fort to live elsewhere." A sob shook him, and an otherworldly, heartbroken wail rang out.

Out of the corner of her eye, Essie saw Sharon start shaking. She wrapped her arms around Sharon and held on. The story wasn't over. More outbursts of tears and eerie noises were possible.

Captain Fremont started pacing again. "I couldn't believe it. Not her! She promised to wait for me!" The captain stopped. His eyes burned red with hate as he put his hand on his sword. "My heart was never the same after that. It turned hard. If the admiral hadn't sent me on that last voyage, I'd have been married to my love. It was his fault she disappeared."

His crew let out an angry yell.

The captain seemed to grow larger. "The admiral took her away from me. He had to pay. And pay he did. I robbed his treasures. I sank his ships. I killed his men."

Essie put a hand over her mouth to control the gasp.

"For years, we waged war against each other. Then we met in battle. I told my men to take him alive. I needed to know where my sweetheart was, but I never had a chance to ask. He went down with his ship."

He puffed up with pride and nodded at his cheering crew. "She promised to wait for me at the White House Inn! She's here somewhere and I'll find her even if I have to look for all eternity! During my mortal life, I never found Adella. I swore I wouldn't rest until I found her in the afterlife. Alas, I haven't found her yet. My ship still sails on the sea. My beautiful Merribelle." Heart-rending, heart-breaking, whining sounds came from the ghostly form as he paced.

Essie felt a small lump in her throat and her eyes burned a little. She quickly wiped her cheeks, surprised to find them moist. She heard a sniff from Sharon as she pulled a tissue from her pocket.

Hannah changed positions on the sofa, taking a more casual posture. "Why aren't you still on your ship, going from port to port looking for her? She's obviously not here. You should run along."

One of his crewmates stepped forward. Dressed better than the other two crewmen, he seemed more confident than the others. "If I may, sir," he said to the captain.

Captain Fremont motioned his permission.

He stepped toward the sisters. "I'm First Mate John Cockarill. I served with the captain for many years and was on our last voyage, as were Clem and Artie." He swept his arm toward his two shipmates. "A few years after we took care of the admiral, we went down in a storm. Down we went with the bulk of the Merribelle, to the bottom of the ocean. Funny thing was, our bodies were dead, but we were still alive. Our ship may be at the bottom of the sea, but it's still alive, out there on the waves. It will come for us when the captain finds Adella McPhee. We've searched every white house along the coast for years, hoping to find her."

Hannah leaned forward in the chair. "You don't know where Adella McPhee is. This cottage isn't the White House Inn. Go look for her elsewhere. If she's not there, keep looking. You know she's not here. Move along."

The captain let out another pitiful cry as John continued. "We went to the inn during every full moon, but she was nowhere to be found. We stayed there for years, too afraid to leave lest she miss us. But a passing fellow mentioned another white house down the way, and Captain Fremont wondered if we were in the right place. Down there we went, looking for her. She wasn't there either. After several years, we moved on to another white house. And another. And another. We know she's joined us in this realm, but where is she? She should have come looking for the captain. Their love was true. She should be looking for him."

Out of the corner of her eye, Essie saw Sharon fidgeting and her mouth moving. She gave Sharon a little nudge so her question would pop out.

"Captain," she began with a squeaky voice, "What if she started going to church and is in Heaven?"

Captain Fremont stopped and stared at Sharon with the icy stare of death. Sharon shrank against Essie and went limp. Essie reached out to grab her before she slid off onto the floor.

The captain bellowed like a foghorn. "I won't stop looking for her until Judgment Day!"

Essie put her hands over her ears, afraid he was going to keep talking at that volume.

"Settle down!" Hannah yelled, rebutting his volume. "There's no need to shout." She sat up on the sofa and put her feet on the coffee table. "Look, we don't care if you keep looking for your lady, but you and your men can't stay here to do it. If she shows up, we'll tell her where you're looking for her." She pointed at her two ghostly friends cringing behind the sofa. "Peg Leg can bring her to you."

Hannah stood and signaled for Essie and Sharon to do the same. "Now, if you'll be on your way, it's been a long night and we'd like to get a little rest."

The captain and his men stood rooted to the spot. His men's eyes darted between the captain and Hannah. The hats were back on their heads, and they raised their fists as if ready to take on a fight.

At last, Captain Fremont let out a low laugh. "I'm not leaving. We'll share the house. We'll use the house at night, and you'll use it during the day. Everyone is happy." He crossed his arms. "What say you to that?"

Essie was tired, her patience ebbing with frustration. The skies were turning gray with the dawn, and she hadn't slept since the night before. "I say no."

Sharon muffled a yawn that swept across the sisters like a virulent virus.

Ignoring the response, Captain Fremont stood. "We're in agreement. Men, let's retire to the attic and lay low while the ladies rest. We'll show them how nice it can be with us sharing the house. Come on, mates, to our new quarters." Slowly, he rose from the floor and floated upwards. "See you this evening!" The others began to follow him upward, passing through the ceiling one by one.

Essie rubbed her eyes, hoping everything was a dream, and she'd wake up at home in her own bed. Looking around, she knew the nightmare continued. How could she sleep with ghosts in the attic? How did she know they wouldn't come snooping around when she was sleeping? She looked at the droopy eyes of Sharon. It didn't matter, as long as they could rest.

Peg Leg and Rummy Jones started upward. "I want to talk to you two!" Hannah said to them before they went far.

They took off their hats and looked sheepishly at Hannah. "Want to tell me how those pirates came to be here?"

Sharon went to the overstuffed chair and sat. Her frown matched her voice tone. "Why'd you let them in here? I thought you were guarding the place?"

Peg Leg looked at his foot that was turned inward and twisted his toe into the floor. "You can see how he is. We didn't ask them in. They came in on their own."

"Long time ago," Rummy Jones said, "we was on his ship. Me and Peg thought they would stay for just one night or two, but they liked it here and decided to stay for good."

Essie was losing her fear of ghosts, especially these two patsies. They seemed as fearful of the captain as she was. She stepped up and said, "And didn't you ask them to leave?"

Rummy Jones answered, "Oh yes, ma'am, we did. Maybe not asked 'em, but hinted at it. Hinted at it a lot."

Sharon piped in. "You should have done more than hint. Tell them. Tell them they have to go! If you did, they would."

Essie moved to sit on the sofa and put her feet on the coffee table. She closed her eyes and rubbed them again. She said a mental apology to her mother. No one was respecting her furniture.

Fatigue was fogging Essie's brain so much nothing made sense anymore. Her body begged for sleep. But first, she had to support her sisters. "Look, insist that they leave. Be assertive about it. Go with them and help them in their search for this lady."

Rummy Jones looked frightened. "No, ma'am, we can't do that."

"Why not? Won't Captain Fremont listen to you? What makes you hesitate to ask him to leave?"

Hannah asked, "How did you come to know him?"

Peg Leg and Rummy Jones looked at each other, then at their feet. Rummy Jones spoke, "We ain't too proud of us on tha'un."

Essie waited for more, but the ghosts kept staring at their feet. Impatient for an end to the conversation, she prodded them on, "You're pirates. I'd think you have lots you're not proud of."

Hannah slapped the sofa with her fist. "Out with it! I don't have the patience for games! Tell us why you're so afraid of Captain Fremont! If you don't, so help me, I'll have Headless here with his hellhounds tomorrow!"

Peg Leg waved his hands in front of him. "No! No hellhounds! Tell 'em, Rum!"

The ghost pirate looked at the three women. When his eyes rested on Essie, she returned his gaze with one of her looks she gave her children when they hadn't done what they told them. When his eyes widened, she knew the look had had its desired effect.

Rummy Jones lifted his shoulders in a shrug and pressed his lips together. After a few minutes of fidgeting, he said, "Okay, I'll tell you, but you must promise me, you won't make us do anything to upset the captain. He could do terrible things to us. Promise me!"

Essie looked at her sisters. They looked as tired as she felt. Not feeling up to additional argument, she said, "Okay, we won't tell anyone about what you're going to share with us."

Still looking at his feet, Rummy Jones told them, "Me and Peg sailed with the cap'n one time and found out where he hid his booty. After we left his crew," he stuffed his hands in his pockets, "we made our way back there and got a little of it."

"Not all of it!" Peg Leg interjected.

Rummy Jones nodded. "Only enough to keep us in rum and women for a while. Or what we thought was enough. Us and money, we don't stick together too long. It was gone fast. But we knowed where there'uz more. We went back and got a little more."

"Not all of it!" Peg Leg interjected again.

"No, we didn't take it all, just what we needed. But I

guess over time, we took more than we shoulda. Cap'n Fremont seen his treasure was going down. We was going back for the last time when he caught us."

"It was bound to have happened sooner or later," Sharon said as she yawned. "What happened after that?"

Rummy Jones jumped in. "As you can imagine, the ol' cap'n was pretty mad at us. Why he—"

Peg Leg nudged Rummy Jones with his elbow. "I was telling this story!" He turned back to the ladies. "He was mad at us all right. So mad that he—well, he made us into ghosts."

"What?" Essie's voice rang out louder than she intended. "He made you into ghosts? Is that what you said?" She was fully awake, adrenaline shooting through her.

"He killed you?" Hannah asked, seeming as awake as Essie was.

Rummy Jones was nodding his head as Peg Leg said, "Yep, he run us through with his sword. We died right there in that cave. His crew dumped our bodies into the sea."

Rummy Jones added, "T'wasn't that bad. Better'n being buried under dirt. I love the sea. I'm happy my body is there still."

Essie's mouth went dry. Happy? Ghosts had feelings about where their bodies are buried? He wasn't distressed over being murdered. He was happy he'd been buried at sea. He was a strange guy but seemed nice enough. For a ghost anyway.

Essie rubbed her forehead. What was she thinking? The ghosts weren't people, although they used to be. This was too weird for her to handle in her fatigued state.

Sucking in a huge breath of air, Hannah let it out slowly as she asked, "Sooo, Captain Fremont killed you for taking his loot. Not surprising. Captains are very possessive of their treasures." She rubbed her temples. "You should have had more sense than to take it."

Peg Leg crunched his small hat in his hands. "Yes, ma'am. I'm not known for having many brains. But no matter, me and Rum here, we live on without our bodies. It's cheaper too. Don't have to pay room or board or buy food. But I do miss the rum."

Essie expressed the question that had been bugging her since this conversation began, "If you're dead, how can Captain Fremont hurt you? What else can he do to you?"

Rummy Jones rushed behind Peg Leg, holding him as a barrier between him and the questioner. "Terrible things!"

Surprised at the response, Essie continued, "But you're dead. What's worse than that?"

Sharon nodded, obviously wanting to know the same thing.

Peg Leg leaned in. "He knows Lucifer himself. If we cross him, he'll send us straight to the lake of fire. Please, don't make us send him away!"

Now Essie had heard it all. The ghosts were afraid of going to hell. No wonder they were reluctant to ask them to leave the cottage. They were no different than anyone else would feel. But they were pirates. With the robbing and pillaging, where'd they think they'd end up? Sooner or later, they'd have to go there. But what if they were good pirates? Would they go there? Too much to think of, and it wasn't her problem.

Hannah sat back in the overstuffed chair and looked at the ceiling where their paranormal guests were. "Still, you're at fault for them being here. You have to help us get rid of them."

Peg Leg let out a cynical laugh. "Twouldn't do no good. He don't listen to us."

"Now what?" Sharon and Essie added their concurrences in unison.

"We don't know," Rummy Jones said, crumpling his hat in his hands. "You need to learn to live with them. They ain't so bad ifn you get to know them."

The sounds of birds and road traffic drifted in the still open front door. Orange and bright yellow clouds reflected some of their brilliance through the kitchen window, giving a soft ambience to the room. In the distance somewhere, a rooster crowed to welcome the day.

The long time without sleep was taking its toll on Essie. The wall of social politeness broke and a wall of impatience and frustration roared out. "No!" she yelled. "I don't want to share the cottage with pirates! Not even you two!" She shook her fist at the ceiling. "All of you, get out!"

Peg Leg put on his hat and strode around the end of the sofa. The silent grandfather clock was visible through him. "Ya not be the boss of us. Mister Horseman asked us here, and it be his word we listen to." He took a stride toward Essie.

She pushed herself back into the cushion of the chair. She might not be as scared of him as she was of the others, but he still put the fear in her.

Hannah waved her hand as she yawned. "Enough of this!" She stabbed a finger at Peg Leg. "You let them in. You get them out. The sun is almost up. Go to the attic and let us rest. Get out of here!"

With a tip of his hat, Peg Leg floated to the ceiling, pulling Rummy Jones along with him. After they disappeared through the ceiling, Essie leaned her head against the back of the chair and closed her eyes. In the few seconds before she drifted off to sleep, she heard the heavy breathing of her sisters. They'd beaten her to sleep by seconds.

Chapter 6

Sharon

Sharon's aching back awoke her. Prying her eyes open, a few moments passed before she remembered where she was and why she was sitting in the overstuffed chair. Soft snoring was the only sound in the room. She struggled to sit up straighter. The backs of her knees hurt from having her feet on the coffee table so long, and her feet were numb. She rubbed her legs until the tingling stopped.

Pulling her cell phone out of her pocket, she checked the time. Two thirty! They'd slept all day!

Essie stirred, mumbled something in her sleep, and was still again.

Sharon limped and stumbled into the kitchen. The smell of coffee would rouse her sisters. Opening the cupboards and refrigerator, she looked for anything to eat. Her stomach rumbled in excitement at being fed.

When the sisters left the cottage the previous fall, Sharon had used most of the perishables in the refrigerator. Only a few canned goods were in the cabinets, but luckily, a partial can of coffee was left. Starting the coffee, she sorted through the pantry looking for any idea for a meal. Canned soup? No. Beans? Never! Flour, sugar, and spices were stored in plastic containers in the pantry, and she found butter in the freezer. Looking behind a container of rice, she found an unopened bottle of syrup. Pancakes! They were better with bacon or fresh fruit, but she had neither. Plain would have to do. Not that nutritious, but better than being hungry.

In a few minutes, the smell of coffee permeated the cottage, beckoning the living residents in the cottage to come and have some. The sound of stirring in the living room grew louder.

Essie was the first one to stagger into the kitchen to sit at the eating bar. "What would we do without you to cook for us," she said in a scratchy morning voice as Sharon poured her a cup of coffee.

"You'd have to do it yourself," Sharon said as she poured a mug for Essie.

Hannah yawned and stretched as she came in the kitchen. Sharon poured her a mug of coffee too.

"I'm making pancakes because that's all there was to cook. We should rent a car and do a little shopping. Ghosts may not have to eat, but I do. We can find an all-night grocery store and stock up. Getting groceries will give us something to do after nightfall. I have a feeling we won't be sleeping too much while we're here."

Hannah shook her head. "We're not going to be here that long. No sense buying food we won't eat."

Essie combed her hair with her fingers. "We must get those ghosts out of here," she said as she smoothed her wrinkled clothes. "Otherwise I can't bring my family here. I don't want my children exposed to pirates and their morals. Or rather their lack of them."

Sharon knew that was important, but other things mattered more. She whispered, "What about visiting Mother? We have two more visits with her."

Hannah put down her coffee cup that was half full and whispered, "We shouldn't call her back with our uninvited guests around. I don't even want our two worthless security guards to be here when we call her. We must wait until they leave to set the clock to bring her back. If these pirates," —she looked around and lowered her voice to a whisper— "If they knew what the clock does, they might create all kinds of havoc while she's here. Or they might use it to call her back once we're gone."

Sharon's heart fluttered. If they called her, she and her sisters would miss an opportunity to be with their mother again. Maybe they might call her father. He wouldn't be happy if someone other than his daughters summoned him. They had to protect the clock's magic from the unscrupulous pirates.

Essie cleared her throat. "I agree with your idea of being cautious, but Mother or Father could likely help us. She's on the same side of death as they are. She could give the word, and they'd have to leave. That would take the burden off Rummy Jones and Peg Leg."

Sharon brought the coffee pot over and refilled their cups. "Father didn't say anything about a limit on the number of times we can call him. He's wise and may know of a way to get rid of them."

Hannah let out a cry like an exasperated teenager. "Listen to yourselves! When we got here last night, you were scared to death of them and now you're calling them friends." She rolled her eyes as she took a sip of coffee.

Sharon tapped the end of the spatula on the counter while she counted to ten. Being made fun of raised her irritation level. "Glad we amuse you. I admit I was scared at first, especially of the captain, but seeing how you acted around them, Hannah, made me realize I didn't need to be." She flipped the first pancakes on the sizzling grill. They released a pleasant aroma around the kitchen. Wagging the turner in the air, she continued, "And they made me mad about not leaving. I guess anger makes me a little braver."

Essie pushed her cup toward Sharon, signaling the request for more coffee. "I know what you mean. I was scared, but when we had that long conversation with the captain, I realized they were like regular people. They still give me the creeps, but I can handle that." The sound of her stomach growling for food caused the sisters to giggle.

"I usually don't eat pancakes," Hannah said, patting her flat stomach. "They have too many carbs. But I might make an exception today."

"It's either this or go hungry. There's nothing in the refrigerator to cook with." Gathering the first short stack, Sharon set it in front of Essie. She poured another set of smaller pancakes on the hot griddle. The sound of the sizzling batter and the smell made her impatient for her own short stack, but first she'd feed her sisters. "I'll make a shopping list, but how long do you think we'll be here?"

Sharon's question floated in the air before landing with a thud. The truth couldn't be denied. This was not an overnight trip unless they wanted to cede the cottage to the ghosts. The power of the clock prevented her from walking away from the cottage and their parents. Santa wouldn't be coming to get them for a while.

With her heart at the bottom of her stomach, Sharon said, "I'll get enough for several days." She flipped the pancakes. "I think we should call Father back. He said to call him if we needed help with anything."

Hannah shushed Sharon. "No," she whispered, looking at the ceiling for eavesdroppers. "If they see how to call him, they'll be calling him all the time. He'll quit coming because he won't know if it's us or those silly ghosts calling. Mother said he would come when he could and not for long. Let's don't waste his time."

She took a big bite of pancakes, closed her eyes, and smiled slightly. "Yum, Sharon! Thanks for cooking. I didn't realize how hungry I was."

Even the compliment couldn't cheer Sharon. The tug of home was too strong. She flipped the pancakes on the griddle. "What can we do? Is there such a thing as a ghost exterminator? You know, where they spray for them or something?"

Essie stopped chewing to stare at Sharon.

Sharon looked at Hannah who had a blank look on her face.

"Are you serious?" Hannah asked in a partly laughing, but mostly mocking tone.

Sharon slammed the pancakes down on a plate and slid them across the counter to Hannah. The plate went too far, but Essie stopped it before it went off the edge. Essie put the plate gently in front of a glaring Hannah.

"Let's not start down the hostile road again," Essie said as she continued to eat her pancakes like a starving woman. "We'll get nothing done if we do," she continued with a full mouth.

Sharon resigned herself to Essie's advice. No sense dwelling on Hannah's terseness. Chalk it up to fatigue and stress.

As she poured the last of the pancake batter on the grill, she glanced at her currently overbearing sister as she buried her short stack under an inordinate amount of syrup. The brown, gooey blanket went across the top of the stack and down the sides like a waterfall. A brown lake formed on the plate. An ocean of carbs for someone who didn't like them.

Seeing that raised Sharon's irritation another level. How could she eat like that and stay thin? It wasn't fair.

Hoping there would be enough syrup left for her own stack, she turned back to the stove and flipped the pancakes.

"Any other ideas about getting rid of them?" Essie said with her last mouthful of pancakes.

Sharon rubbed her weary eyes. "The only thing I can think of is asking a priest to come do an exorcism."

"They're not demons!" Hannah cried out. "They're obnoxious ghosts who won't leave when asked." The sound of footsteps sounded on the ceiling. "Keep your voices down. They may be listening."

Essie pushed back the curtains to let in the bright, afternoon sun into the kitchen. "What are we going to do while they have full run of the house?"

Sharon sat at the counter with her own pancakes, pouring what was left of the syrup over them. "We can't stay here. I may be brave, but I'm not that brave. With ghosts dancing around all night, how could I sleep? It's midafternoon, and they'll be taking over soon. I'm tired. I'm sleepy. I'm messed up!" Her breath started getting shorter and her chest was tighter. She felt the anxiety level creeping up. Her paper bag was on the countertop, ready and close by for her use. She grabbed it and held it to her face.

Hannah calmly drank a sip of coffee and said, "We could sleep on the beach tonight. There's blankets in the closet and the sand should be warm. We used to do that as children. How about reliving childhood days for one night?"

"I'm okay with sleeping outside," Essie added. "How about you, Sharon?"

"I don't want to stay here, but I don't want to turn the house over to them. We could get a little of Mother's money out to pay for a hotel room."

Hannah got up to get another cup of coffee. "We can't touch that money. You know how pirates love loot and if they knew it was there, who knows what they'd do."

A phone rang. Essie got her phone out of her pocket and went into the living room. From the one side of the discussion heard, her children were missing her and wanted her to come home.

Sharon took a bite of her pancakes. The sugar kicked in and perked her up a little. A sip of coffee brought her closer to logical thinking. "I'm not much for sleeping outside, but it's better than staying in here. We could rent another tent like the last time. Or pool our money and buy a camping tent."

Hannah nodded as she ate the last of her stack. "First, we should call the sheriff and tell him we're here checking on things. They might think three hobos have moved into the neighborhood if they see us out there."

Sharon had to put her fork down for a moment. "That still doesn't help us with how to get rid of Captain Fremont and his gang." Her heart was overwhelmed with butterflies and her breathing was coming more quickly.

Hannah pushed the paper bag toward her.

Sharon touched it, but hesitated. Why did she have to

be this way? Everything here scared her. She was very uncomfortable in her childhood home. She'd faced ghosts last night and survived. She could face them again if she could only get over the anxiety overloads.

She moved the bag beside her but didn't use it. "Let's sleep on the beach, but first, can we go to the store?"

In the cloudless skies that night, the stars twinkled as if they were winking at the absurdity of her plight. Boat lights in the distance reflected in the calm sea. The surf sang its lullaby of white noise to block out the music coming from the cottage. No moaning or other unearthly sounds were heard that night.

Hannah helped Sharon dig out a comfy spot in the sand for a bed. She was so tired she could have slept on gravel and not felt it. She pulled the blanket up around her face to shield it from the cool breeze and slept deeply, more from exhaustion than comfort.

She woke when she tried to turn over. The sand wasn't as comfortable as her bed back home. The side of her face was gritty. Sand trickled down the leg of her capris and up her sleeves to access places where it was not welcome.

The gray sky of morning signaled their shift in the cottage would begin soon. She felt grungy. Her muscles ached all over. Her eyes still burned with the need for more sleep, but her busy mind wouldn't let it come.

Hannah lay to her right, motionless. Essie, on her left, moved occasionally.

Sharon willed herself to lie still, but her mind refused to be idle. What was she doing sleeping in the sand and talking to ghosts? The elves and Santa were in their cozy beds at home. If the ghosts hadn't come, she'd be there too.

The yearning to be at home, safe in her little stone house on the icecap, grew stronger. A definite date for return would help her get through the next few days. The tyrannosaurus rex of homesickness was hot on her heels and about to swallow her whole.

Essie turned and shuffled around. "Sharon, are you awake?" Essie whispered, pulling Sharon out of her thoughts.

"Yes, I can't sleep."

"Me neither. I had an idea." Essie turned on her side to face Sharon. "I wonder if we could find Captain Fremont's girlfriend. If we found her, we could bring her back here. She might persuade him to call his ship and they'd sail away and leave us alone."

Sand must be in her ears because Sharon couldn't believe the words coming out of her sister. "What did you say? We should go looking for a ghost?"

"Yes! Let's go find her. It's better than waiting for him to do it. He's been looking for what, a century? He needs help with it."

Sharon's heart picked up its pace. "I think that's a great idea except for one thing. How do we find a ghost? Especially a ghost named Adella McPhee?"

Essie shrugged her shoulder not sticking in the sand. "No idea, but she may be the only one he'll listen to. He said if he found her, he'd leave. I know he's a dishonest scoundrel, but where love is involved, he'll probably keep his word. If you have any better ideas, please say so."

Sharon let out a wistful sigh, longing for the problem to disappear. Desperation was closing her throat. Her mind was overloaded. Too much supernatural stuff. Santa was a supernatural being because he would live forever. But he was supernatural in a good and jolly way. Dealing with the ghostly and mischievous supernatural made her anxiety levels spin out of control.

Taking a slow deep breath, she held it a moment before exhaling it. "Other than calling a priest, I'm not sure what else to do. It's the best idea we got, and I think Hannah will go along with it."

Essie started to rise out of the sand. "Of course, she will." She checked her watch. "It's a little after four. The sun will come up soon, and they'll go back to the attic. Let's go talk to Captain Fremont to see if he'll agree to leave if we find his true love. If not, we'll call a priest or a witch doctor or whatever it takes to get him out of Mother's house." Essie got up out the sand, holding onto her back with each phase of rising.

Sharon's anxiety kicked up a notch. "Shouldn't we ask Hannah to go along with us?"

Essie shook her head. "We can do it without her. Let her sleep."

The sand had a strong grip on Sharon and was reluctant to cooperate as she tried to rise. Loose sand had blown over her during the night and filled her clothes. Getting off the ground wasn't something she did often. Her muscles didn't want to work right, and her efforts to rise were mostly unsuccessful until Essie reached under her arm and helped boost her out of the sand.

A phone rang. Sharon knew it wasn't hers. She brushed the sand out of her hair and her clothes while Essie whispered to one of her children it wasn't a good time to talk and to get the chores done whether her sister helped or not.

Hanging up, Essie muttered something under her breath.

Sharon didn't want to know about it. She had enough on her mind to worry about.

Hobbling along, the two sisters made their way to the cottage. Sharon felt her heart pounding, and her skin tingled with apprehension as she climbed the three steps to the porch. Her paper bag was somewhere, but she wasn't sure where. Probably out under her blanket on the beach. No place she could get to quickly. Essie would have to be her shield. Otherwise, she might pass out from the fright. Hannah could do this better than either of them. Why let her sleep?

"Are you sure we should do this without Hannah? She knows how to handle them. Without her, you'll have to do all the talking because I certainly can't."

Essie spun to glare at her cowering sister. "What happened to the courage you had last night when you stood up to them?"

A loud moan made its way through the door sending a cold fear through Sharon. She ran down the steps and out into the yard. Her breathing pushed too much oxygen into her lungs. Her head spun. Where was her bag? She needed her bag. Placing her hands over her face and nose like a bag, her breathing needed to slow.

While concentrating on regaining control, she felt a hand on her back.

Essie whispered in her ear, "They dishonor our mother's memory by refusing to leave. You saw what they did to her furniture. We can't let that happen. For Mother's sake, we have to defend her home." Her mother's home. It was rightly theirs. The ghosts were squatters. Trespassers who needed to move on. If only Hannah was here instead of her.

Essie whispered again, "You coming with me?"

Sensing her sister's courage, Sharon exhaled as much fear as she could. There was no other choice. She had to support her sister. She had to uphold her mother's memory. Holding her breath to stop the swirling in her brain, she grasped a tiny thread of courage and turned toward the cottage.

Essie's hand trembled as she turned the doorknob. With a creak, the door swung open. In the dim light, they saw two ghost pirates doing a jolly dance on top of the coffee table as music blared from a clock radio they'd brought into the living room. Their boots made tapping sounds on the tabletop as they danced. The others stood around the table clapping, stomping their feet, and letting out an occasional howl. Rummy Jones and Peg Leg stood in the hallway clapping along. The dancing pirates didn't lose a beat when the sisters entered, but instead waved at them to join in the dance on the table top.

Sharon shrunk back behind Essie, fighting the urge to run. Her shield needed to be bigger.

Essie was trembling more than before, but her voice was firm as she shouted above the din, "We'd like to talk to you, Captain Fremont."

The overstuffed chair had been pushed into the corner by the clock where the captain sat like a king on his throne holding court. He waved at Essie from the far side of the room, but made no move to stop the commotion or to come to them.

"I need to talk to you!"

The party continued.

Seeing the problem, Sharon crept over to the clock radio sitting on the eating bar and turned it off. An instant of silence was flooded by loud eerie moaning, filling the room as much as the music had a second earlier. One short ghost pirate started toward her, and her heart nearly stopped beating. She picked up the radio and ran behind Essie. Shutting her eyes, she didn't want to see what would happen next.

"What'd you do that for?" the captain roared. "You've interrupted our party."

"We need to talk to you," Essie said as loudly. "It's almost sunup. Party time is almost over anyway. It's time to talk."

"You be wanting to parlay?" Captain Fremont said as he rose from his throne and came closer.

"Yes," Essie said, backing up into Sharon behind her.

Sharon stood firm. As long as Essie was her shield, she'd make sure Essie stood her ground.

Essie's voice trembled, but she didn't retreat. "I wanted to know—"

Behind the sisters, a figure darkened the door. "What's going on here?" Hannah asked in a voice of fire and ice. "Why didn't someone wake me? What are you two doing here without me?" Her glare at her sisters made Sharon more scared of her than the captain.

"We had an idea about resolving our dilemma," Essie told her like a child caught playing with matches.

"Essie had a question for the captain," Sharon added, deflecting the anger toward her quivering sister. "I'm here for moral support."

Essie gave Hannah a go-with-me-on-this look. She spoke to Hannah out of the side of her mouth in a low voice. "We were wondering if we found this Adella McPhee, would he be willing to leave."

Captain Fremont took a step closer. "What did ya say?" He cocked his head as if trying to peer inside their minds.

Sharon stepped back behind Essie and Hannah. They could deal with the ghost captain. She was content to let them take charge. She glanced at Hannah, who had the same expression on her face as the captain had. A light bulb flickered to life.

After a slight nod from Hannah, Essie continued quietly. "We wondered if we find out what happened to Adella McPhee, would you leave? No matter what we find out, would you call your ship and leave our house never to come back?"

Folding his arms, Captain Fremont said, "What makes you think you can find her? I've been looking for many years and couldn't. What makes you special?"

Sharon peeked out from behind Essie. "You—you—you—" she cleared her throat, hoping to choke up some courage and poise— "you see, we heard paranormal hunters wanted to meet with us. Maybe they know where she is. We can ask them for you."

John came up beside the captain. "What's a paranormal hunter? I never heared of paranormals."

An uncontrolled giggle came from Sharon as Hannah answered, "You are paranormals. They're people who look for ghosts."

His eyebrows shot up as Captain Fremont stroked his beard. Once again, he took his Superman stance. "You proposing to look for my true love?" His three ghost friends gathered around him. "Wha'da'ya think, men? Would we go if the ladies found my Adella?" The pirates around him let out a mighty roar, and the captain joined in with them.

Behind the group, Peg Leg and Rummy Jones cheered along.

Hannah called for calm and quiet. "That's not what we said. We said if we find out what happened to her, you must go. We cannot guarantee we can find her or that she will want to go with you. That will be between the two of you."

A frown came across the captain's face. He stroked his beard as he slowly tromped back to the overstuffed chair and sat down. The cold glare at the sisters gave Sharon the shivers. The air inside the cottage seemed icy.

"Are we in agreement?" Hannah inquired. "It's a reasonable expectation. If we give you what you want, you give us what we want. You find out what happened to her. What you do with that information is up to you. I don't care as long as you leave this cottage."

The pirates hushed and milled around the captain, whispering things in his ears. He waved them back. He blinked more than he should have before saying softly, "Aye, I need to know what happened to her. I want to see the sweet face of my Adella McPhee, but if she be at Heaven's Gate, I won't call her back." He cleared his throat. "I must also consider my men who have stood by me in life and in death. They deserve women of their own to spend eternity with." A snakelike smile spread across his face. "I'll agree to your terms IF you find my Adella and some of her friends."

Beside the captain, John had a wry smile on his face, and Clem and Artie stood behind him, grinning and rubbing their hands together.

Sharon quickly grabbed her sisters and huddled with them. "Is this our only option? How are we going to find Adella, much less lady ghosts that want to spend eternity with scroungy pirates?"

Worry wrinkled Essie's brow as she shook her head. "It's the only glimmer of hope we've had since we got here."

Hannah nodded. "If he agrees to this plan, he must abide by it. We'll find a way to make it work. We have to! Are we agreed?"

Sharon quickly gave her consent, but she had her unspoken doubts.

Breaking the huddle, Hannah turned to face the captain. "It's a deal. We find Adella McPhee and her friends, and you leave never to return." She walked over to him and held out her hand.

Captain Fremont looked at it for a moment, then reached out his own hand. They shook, and the deal was sealed.

Feeling relieved and more scared than ever, Sharon felt a flicker of hope. Or was it panic? All they had to do was find Adella McPhee and friends.

Chapter 7

Hannah

"Mom, when are you coming home? You've been gone forever."

Huntley's voice made Hannah's heart cringe. Rubbing her still-sleepy eyes, she replied, "It's been two days. That's a short forever."

An exasperated moan sounded from the phone. "You know what I mean. I need you to come home, so you can take me to baseball practice."

"Why can't Mrs. Hagg take you?"

The volume of the outcry made Hannah drop her phone and rub her ear. His exaggerated cry was familiar, coming whenever he didn't get his way. No sense in reprimanding him for it. It was a harmless way for him to release his frustrations. Releasing her own building frustrations with a primal scream might feel good. Later.

A tiny voice came from the phone. She quickly picked it up. she didn't want to miss what he was saying.

"Because the guys make fun of me when she takes me. You know what her car looks like. That smoky, loud piece of moving rust. Everyone hears it come up and when I get out, they start laughing at me. She's embarrassing me! Please, Mom, you have to come home so she doesn't take me to practice anymore. It'll ruin my life if you don't."

Those words. The ruination of his life. They weren't a

new threat, but an often quoted one. His life had been ruined many times before, yet he seemed to live through it. This time would be no different, but that didn't keep her guilt away. Being home to take him to baseball practice was her greatest wish too. But it wasn't going to happen.

"Tell Mrs. Hagg to drive my car when she takes you to practice. They won't notice it's not me."

A quieter cry came through the phone. At least she'd made him think about it.

"They'll know it's her. She doesn't look like you at all."

"It's the best I can do from here, sweetheart. I can't come home yet, but I'll be there as soon as I can."

"Can I tell Dad to come take care of it. Styx and Shuck would get rid of Rummy Jones and Peg Leg for you."

Her heart ached to tell him yes. "It's more complicated than that." As she explained the pirate situation to him, the doorbell rang. Knowing her sisters would take care of the visitor, she ignored it and continued to talk to her son until a pounding on the door stopped their conversation.

In a flurry of her red and black sundress, Sharon rushed through her bedroom door. "Sorry to bother you. Some women and a sheriff's deputy are here to complain about the noise at the house. They look mad." She looked in the closet until she found Hannah's robe and held it out for her.

"Huntley, I have to go. Call me after practice tonight and tell me how it went." She hung up and waved Sharon out of the room. "If we have visitors, I'll put more than a robe on. Now shoo."

As Hannah dressed, she heard voices in the living room, some high-pitched and anxious, others low pitched and angry. Rather than putting on her blue shirt, she opted to wear solid black. More intimidating. Ghosts were hard to deal with, but people were much harder and more unpredictable. She put on a little makeup to complete the look and went into the living room.

The police officer stood near the front door, hands on his well-equipped gun belt. Hannah remembered his face from his visit after they ran Howie Howard off. Officer Stanus, if she remembered his name right. On the edges of the sofa, two purse-lipped, raised-eyebrowed ladies sat erect. Their polyester outfits and sensible shoes could be found in any senior center. When Hannah entered the room, the women looked her over like she had a bullseye on her shirt.

A smile formed inside Hannah, but her demeanor did not reflect her inner amusement. These must be the neighbors who had complained to the police about the cottage. Deflecting the daggers they brought with them would be an interesting exercise.

Sharon stood at the edge of the kitchen wringing her hands, her normally warm hospitality chilled by the icy stares of the visitors on the sofa.

Essie came toward Hannah, making a horrendous face seen only by her sister right before putting on her sweetest smile. She turned and presented Hannah to the frosty pair on the sofa. "This is my sister, Hannah. Hannah, this is Estelle Moltz and Cathy Franks. They're our neighbors."

Mumbled greetings sufficed for the niceties.

Still feeling a little miffed at having her call with Huntley disturbed, Hannah asked, "You feel it necessary to come visit with an armed escort?"

Beside her, Essie took in a sharp breath. "But wasn't it nice for them to come over. They're the first neighbors to come visit."

Sharon rushed from her spot by the kitchen. "I'm sorry I haven't had time to bake cookies to offer you. I've been busy with things since we arrived and haven't had time to bake. Can I get you coffee or tea or water or—"

Estelle held her hand up. "Nothing, thank you. We're here on business. Our escort, as you refer to him, is here to make sure we're safe. We weren't sure what kind of reception we'd get. I mean, the house seems…hostile."

"I assure you—" Sharon sputtered, "—we are the

nicest people. You had no reason to be afraid. Did they, sisters."

Essie immediately agreed.

Hannah nodded. No need to grovel to the old biddies. They were obviously the ones who complained to the police about the cottage. They were the reason she had to be here away from her family. "I'm pretty sure this isn't a 'welcome to the neighborhood' visit. Why don't we get down to business."

The visitors looked at each other before Estelle continued, "We'd like for you to keep the noise level down. It's disrupting the peace and quiet of the neighborhood."

Cathy interjected, "And the blinking lights keep me awake." The visitors nodded at each other, agreeing in what was being said.

Cathy smoothed her blouse. "Please stop renting your house out as a party place or whatever it is that you do that causes such a disturbance."

Estelle waved her thin finger in the air. "Or if it's haunted, we expect you to get those spirits exorcised. Bad spirits don't make good neighbors." The two ladies nodded at each other again.

A stomp on the ceiling caused the visitors to jump and look at the ceiling. Officer Stanus put his hand on his gun but didn't pull it from the holster. "Is anyone up there?"

Looking at the ceiling, Hannah replied, "Just ghosts." With hardly a pause, she yelled out, "Quiet up there!" Ignoring the sharp looks from her sisters, she went on to explain, "As you can hear, the place is haunted. We didn't know they'd moved in until we heard from the sheriff."

Officer Stanus walked to the middle of the room and looked up. "I figured as much. Too many odd things happening around here to explain it any other way."

Her eyes still on the ceiling, Cathy asked, "What do you plan to do about it?"

"Ghosts run property values down," Estelle spat out. "This will hurt all of us. I know a priest we can call to—"

"No!" Essie and Sharon said together.

Hannah waved her hand to disperse the tense vibes in the room. "Calm down! We're working on it. Give us a few days to get this in hand. Trust me. They'll leave, and tranquility will return to the neighborhood."

Regaining his official composure, Officer Stanus reached in his shirt pocket and pulled out a business card. "The sheriff said to give you this. It's from those ghost hunter guys who want to come explore your house. They can lend a hand in ridding you of these pests."

Another stomp on the ceiling brought a quick end to the social visit. The ladies headed toward the door, ignoring Sharon's invitation to come back later.

After taking the business card from Officer Stanus, Hannah escorted their guests to the door. With a final wave, she shut the door and leaned against it. Turning around, she faced her dumbfounded sisters. "That went well, don't you think?"

A black cargo van was parked outside the cottage when the sisters arrived back from renting a car and running errands. A tattooed, biker-looking man sat on the front porch swing, engrossed in his cell phone. A tall, dark-headed man left the porch as soon as Essie turned off the convertible. A younger, beach-bum-looking man came up from the beach as they got out.

"Hello!" called the dark-headed man. "We've been waiting for you."

"Obviously," Hannah said. The word exited her mouth more sarcastically than she meant. She felt Sharon jab her in the ribs and resisted the urge to jab back. "Who are you and how long have you been here?"

Beach Bum reached out to take the grocery sacks from Sharon and carry them to the cottage.

The dark-haired man walked with the ladies to the porch. "You called us this morning. We're the paranormal explorers. I'm Jeff Campbell, this is Rusty Johnson" —he pointed to the tattooed biker on the swing— "and Clay Allen."

The suntanned, younger man swung the grocery bags in greeting.

"We came as soon as we could get our gear together. From what you said, you think your cottage is haunted. We can help you find out for sure. Tonight, we could set up our cameras to see if we can catch any activity. We can determine if it's haunted or not."

Not wanting another jab in the ribs, Hannah resisted the urge to burst out laughing. To keep it inside, she turned her face to the door as she unlocked it. Opening it up, she walked briskly to the kitchen. The others came in and took seats in the living room.

"There's no if about it," said Essie, as she came in the door. "We know ghosts live here. That's not why we called you."

Stepping inside the cottage, the men exchanged glances. Rusty spoke up from the swing. "You said you need our help. That's what we do. Find out who's haunting you and why they're here. Help them go on to the next life."

Regaining control, Hannah motioned to Clay to take the groceries in the kitchen. Sharon followed him in as Hannah went back to Jeff. "Look, we know who the ghosts are. It's Captain Fremont and his merry band of men, plus a couple of friends of my husband's. They're pirates who lived a long time ago. They're in no hurry to get to the next life because they can already feel the heat of what awaits them."

Three gaping mouths and wide eyes stared at her. Jeff was the first to blink. "Captain Fremont? He's a what?"

Hannah signed for everyone to go back out on the porch. They were already in this far, they might as well go the whole way. Before she followed them, she asked Sharon to bring refreshments out.

The men squeezed themselves onto the porch swing while Essie sat in one of the porch chairs. Sharon came out with a plate full of store-bought cookies and bottled water.

Hannah put one leg up on the railing. She pulled herself up on it like she did when she was younger. The board seemed much smaller. Hanging on the post so she wouldn't fall off, Hannah started the tale. "Our house is haunted by Captain Fremont, an old pirate of these waters, and three of his crew, John, Clem, and Artie. Two other ghosts called Peg Leg and Rummy Jones are here also, but don't worry about them. We need your help with getting rid of the captain and his crew." Unable to stay on the thin seat, Hannah got down.

Essie picked up the story. "They decided to live in our house and won't leave. We talked to the captain and made an agreement. He'll leave if we find his long-lost love, a ghost named Adella McPhee."

Their mouths were still gaping, and their eyes were still wide until Jeff blinked a second time. "Adella who?"

"McPhee. Adella McPhee," Sharon said immediately before she covered her smile with her hand.

Taking a small bite of cookie, Essie added, "She's Captain Fremont's girlfriend." She looked hard at Rusty and waved her hand in front of his face.

He and his compatriots blinked and fidgeted. "Are you okay?" she asked.

The three men came out of their stupor, mumbling amongst themselves. Jeff shushed the others. "That's quite a tale. How do you know this?"

Sharon passed the plate of cookies around. "Captain Fremont told us. I think Essie mentioned it."

The men exchanged glances again. "And you say the ghosts told you this?" He looked at each of them before continuing. "What do you need us for?"

Clay muttered under his breath, "What kind of pills are you taking?" which drew an immediate slap on the back of the head by Rusty.

Fatigue pushed Hannah's anger and impatience up. Why was this incredulous to them? They hunted ghosts for a living, but apparently hadn't run across people who talked to them more than they did.

Biting her lip to keep a bad word from straying out, she paused to calm herself before she told them, "We need your help in finding a ghost named Adella McPhee. Have you ever heard of her or run across her in your paranormal explorations?"

Jeff, Rusty, and Clay traded looks and shrugs. "Can't say that we have," Rusty said.

"But," Clay jumped in, jittery with excitement, "that doesn't mean she's not out there. We must not have looked in the right places. Does the captain know where she might be?" The three men leaned forward, eyes and ears wide open.

The sisters shook their heads and muttered in unison, "No."

Essie waved her sisters off. "She was supposed to wait for him at the White House Inn, but she wasn't there when he returned."

Clay laughed. "That makes it more challenging, but also more fun."

Relieved at the men finally showing interest in working with them, Hannah felt her shoulders relax a little. It didn't matter if the men thought they were crazy. They needed help in finding Adella. Mr. Beach Bum Clay seemed genuinely interested. If they could convince his companions to go along, this idea might work. Their familiarity with the area would help and having a bigger search team meant covering more ground in less time.

Jeff got out of the porch swing and paced up and down the porch. "I'm not sure how we can help. We hunt for ghosts and try to find out who they are. We've never been told they're here and who they are and what they want. I'm not sure how to go about this."

A sniff drew Hannah's eyes to Sharon who sat with shoulders slumped rubbing her eyes. "You won't help us. What do we do now, girls?" Her eyes became sweaty before she rubbed them again.

Taking a handful of cookies from the plate, Clay said,

"Come on, man, we gotta help these ladies."

Jeff stopped in front of Sharon. "I didn't say we wouldn't help. A new situation requires a plan." He stroked his goatee as if extracting ideas. "First, we can send Clay to do some historical research to find records of this Adella McPhee. If we know where she used to live, it'll give us a place to start."

Rusty jumped off the swing. "Before we take off on that, let's back up. Would you ladies mind if we set up our equipment here so we find out this for ourselves? Not that we don't believe you, but we need it for our own research."

Jeff piped in, "We'd pay for you to stay at a hotel for the night. We prefer to have the place to ourselves when we investigate. You see, outside noises sometimes interfere with what we hear on our recordings. It's better if the homeowner goes somewhere else."

Hannah held up her hand and signaled her sisters. "Let us talk about it." They went into the cottage and shut the door. "What do you think?"

Essie whispered, "I love the idea of having a hotel room to ourselves, but let's negotiate for rooms by the pool at the Holiday Inn."

"Beats sleeping in the sand again," Sharon said softly. "As long as they don't touch the clock. They have to promise not to touch it."

Hannah nodded as Essie agreed. "Any other provisions we should put on this agreement? I don't care if they record things in there, but the publicity might bring more of these people here, and we're back to who will take care of the place when we're gone."

Sharon jumped in. "We need a privacy clause. No one knows what goes on here, but them."

Essie looked at the ceiling and whispered, "Do you think the captain will cooperate? These boys would be disappointed if the captain gets uncooperative about it. We should talk to the captain first and get him to agree."

"I'll talk to him. I'm pretty sure he'll agree," Hannah

said. "He'll do it because it means looking for Adella. And the sooner we find her, the sooner we can go home." Hannah rubbed the building stress out of her forehead. Doing research on this Adella might take weeks. She didn't want to be away from her family for that long.

An arm went across her shoulders as she heard Essie say, "I feel the same way. I'm ready to go home too, but what other options do we have? These guys know what they're doing, and it won't take long. It'd take us forever to do the same thing."

Sharon nodded. "They're our best hope. Besides, we'd get to sleep in a hotel!"

Hannah knew there was no sense arguing about it. From the looks on Essie's and Sharon's faces, she'd already lost that battle. She heard an impatient throat clearing from the porch. No use in putting it off any longer. She grabbed her sisters' hands and told them, "We're agreed on the terms. Let's go tell them it's a go and ask if they'll pay for three rooms by the pool."

The sun was high in the sky the next morning when the sisters got back to the cottage, well rested and well fed. They'd taken advantage of the hot tub by the pool and relaxed together, discussing what they'd ask their mother when they called her back. Even though they'd shared a room, the quiet night, soft beds, and showers without the fear of unseen eyes peeking left them feeling refreshed and ready to face the day.

A business card with a note on the back was taped to the front door. Their ghost-hunting guests said they'd had an active night. After getting some sleep, Rusty and Clay would start on the research and get back to them as quickly as possible.

The house seemed to be in order, and the grandfather clock still read nine-fifteen. The furniture was in its proper places. Hannah heard a soft footstep on the ceiling. Their guests were where they belonged for the day.

Essie got out a video of their childhood and put it on. Sitting on the sofa with the extra-large soda she'd brought home with her, she put her feet on the coffee table. As she settled in, her phone rang.

Hannah left her sisters and went to her small bedroom to unpack her suitcase and start a load of laundry. Nothing was left to do, but spend the day doing whatever they wanted. Her deepest wish was to go home to see how her boys were doing with Mrs. Hagg. Had they caused her problems? Were they eating well? Was Huntley still getting teased about who took him to practice?

As she sat on her bed to call home, Rummy Jones floated down from the ceiling. "Hi Rummy," she said to him as he leaned against the wall and crossed his arms. Hannah put her cell phone aside. "Why are you up this time of day?"

"Captain Fremont sent me. He said he did his part, letting them know we was here. He says don't let them come back. It interfered with our fun."

"We thought you'd enjoy helping them with their research. Getting yourselves documented for posterity. Let the world know you're still around."

"Captain Fremont twasn't happy about them being around. He says we want to be left in peace. Says let us do our thing, and we'll let you do yours."

Hannah wagged her finger at him. "Those men are helping us find Adella. You tell the captain he owes them a little haunting in return. Good trade, if you ask me. Besides, we got a free place to stay last night, and it was great. No sand down my pants. No sand in my hair. No waking up to noisy seagulls flying over me."

Rummy Jones stood up straight and put his hands in his pocket. "I'm sorry how this turned out. Mr. Horseman trusted us to watch after this place for you. Me and Peg, we were going to do what he asked. But the captain and his men came in and there tweren't nothing we could do to get them out. You gotta believe me!"

Hannah looked into his transparent, pleading eyes. He

was scared. Of Headless. Of Captain Fremont. Of the hellhounds. Poor guy. Her heart pinged with a touch of compassion.

"I'll make sure Headless knows. Get back to your part of the house so I can call Headless and tell him all is well here. That way he'll quit getting the hellhounds ready to come."

Terror passed across the ghost's face as he slowly rose back through the ceiling.

Chapter 8

Essie

Essie's leg bounced up and down, marking off the passing milliseconds. Essie hated waiting. She always had. Waiting made her feel helpless.

Two days had passed without a call from the ghost guys saying they'd found Adella. Two days with no clue on where to start looking for her. Two days with no hint that they'd even been trying to find her. Two days of nothing. That added to the helpless feeling. There was nothing to do except wait for their research to come up with clues on where to find Adella.

She'd already done everything on her to-do list, and it wasn't lunchtime yet. She'd taken walks on the beach. She'd scrubbed floors. The closets were organized. She wished she hadn't taken so many books home from her last visit. None of the books left behind interested her. Sitting on the porch watching the eternal waves go in and out was her only remaining option.

Her children called often wondering when she was coming home. Several times she'd had to referee an argument. Where was Easter and why wasn't he looking after the kids? She knew. Cleaning up the factory after the Easter deliveries took a lot of time and elbow grease. She should be there to help. To watch over and care for her children. To keep them from making shambles of their house.

She wasn't alone in her misery. Sharon cooked non-stop. It was her stress therapy. When she took her goodies to shelters, she stopped by the stores and bought more ingredients to keep her busy. Much longer and she'd have the state of Florida supplied with cookies, cakes, and bread for the week.

Hannah was bored and wrinkled from long hours of swimming. When she came out of the water, she'd sit under the beach umbrella and stare out to sea. The calls from her boys begging her to come home were hard on her.

The neighbors called every night asking if they'd take care of the blinking lights. Essie had turned off the electricity to the house, but the intruders let out such howls of protestation they had to turn it back on again. Flashing lights were better than the spectral din.

Officer Stanus made another daytime visit to tell them to stop disturbing the peace with the blinking lights. They assured him it wasn't them doing it and they'd take care of it.

How long could this go on?

At mealtimes, the sisters planned on what to do during their mother's upcoming visit. Sharon planned the meals. They weren't sure whether their mother could leave the house, but if so, they'd take a picnic lunch to the beach to watch the ocean, their mother's favorite relaxing activity. Essie organized photos of their children on her phone. She'd share how well they were doing. It would be a perfectly wonderful day.

While sitting alone on the front porch swing, Essie called home and spoke with each of her children to make sure their squabbles had been settled. Alan had the sniffles. Clara liked a boy at school, but he didn't know she was alive. Thomas got a bad grade on a test. Ned fell off a chair and gave himself a black eye. Everyone else was fine. Before closing the calls, their pleading voices asking when she was coming home left her homesick. Afterwards, she stayed alone on the porch with her aching heart.

The smell of fresh cookies wafted its way to the front

porch. Essie knew Sharon had a problem with panic attacks, and baking was her therapy to deal with it. The scales in the bathroom verified the deliciousness and overindulgence in her sister's tasty treats.

The threads of the sisters' relationships had been unraveled for many years. Grudges and silence kept them apart. Their mother's ingenious manipulations had reknit their relationships, and now they were friends. Life was much better with her sisters in it.

All that helped Essie's homesick heart was thinking of her mother. The magic clock would bring her mother back from the Other Side. Sharon had used her turn when they called her the first time. Hannah said she'd share this time with her sisters. The last visit would be courtesy of Essie, and she'd share it with her sisters. How could she not when the others had been generous with their turns. Their mother made a point of spending one-on-one time with whichever daughter summoned her which gave each a chance to say the things they wished they had said before. After her turn, they'd have to say good-bye to their mother until it was their times to pass to the Other Side.

Sharon came outside with a tray of iced tea glasses and cookies. "How're you doing out here? Need a snack?" Her flour-sprinkled apron that declared Baking is My Superpower, What's Yours? covered her denim capris and white shirt. Her red sequined shoes glistened in the sunlight.

Essie waved her to come sit by her on the swing. After she sat, Essie took her sister's hand and squeezed it. "Have I told you how nice it is to have a sister like you? Mother was right in bringing us back together."

Sharon's eyes filled with tears. "What a sweet thing to say!" She lifted Essie's hand and kissed it as Hannah came up from the beach. Laughter joined the sounds of seagulls and surf swirling through the air.

Hannah stopped and stared, eyebrows high. "Am I interrupting a tender moment?"

Essie explained the scene, "We were having a sister moment. I was thinking of how nice it was to have sisters again."

Hannah sat in the white wicker chair, her black swimsuit and coverall a stark contrast. She stared out toward the ocean, her long, dark hair moving with the breeze. "It's true. I couldn't have dealt with these ghosts alone. Or handled Mother's passing without you two here."

"Mother's ploy was a success," Essie admitted to herself as much as to her sisters. "As soon as we get our guests to move along, we can enjoy a visit with her. It will be great."

"But first things first," Hannah said. "Where do we sleep tonight?"

Essie let go of Sharon's hand. Her moment of tranquility and love on the front porch exploded and crashed on the wooden deck. Anxiety filled the void as they discussed sleeping on the beach again.

The sun was touching the horizon when the sisters heard footsteps on the ceiling. Sharon picked up the dishes from the eating counter and took them to the sink. Essie helped her clean the kitchen while Hannah looked on, deep in thought. She hadn't said a word during their supper. Her furrowed brow and staring at the countertop implied her thoughts were heavy and uncomfortable. If she had no hope of getting rid of Captain Fremont and his gang, did that mean all hope was gone? Essie's heart dropped and quickened its beat. They didn't have a Plan B.

As soon as Sharon and Essie had the dishes in the dishwasher, the ghosts started floating down through the ceiling. A few days ago, the sight would have scared her into running out of the house screaming. Now it was like 'ho hum, here they are again.' What was happening to her? She'd become— could it be? —desensitized to ghosts.

"Ahoy, ladies!" Captain Fremont called out when he landed on the floor. "Will ya be joining us tonight?"

His crew let out a loud cheer and waved their hats in

the air, encouraging female company tonight.

Essie joined Sharon in walking past him, going to the door where three small bags awaited them. "No, we are going back to the hotel for another night. Keep it down here, won't you? Don't bother our neighbors with your yowling or light show. They're having a cookout tonight. Please keep it quiet and peaceful here."

Hannah hung back. "Time for another parlay." She seemed cool and calm as she took a seat in the overstuffed chair as the captain and his men circled her in the living room. "I have a proposition for you. We think we've found the perfect place for you to stay until we find Adella. Egmont Key State Park. It's closed at night. You'd be free to party. It's by the ocean. You can keep a weather-eye out for your ship. Don't disturb the visitors by day and roam the whole island at night. We will continue to look for Adella and let you know as soon as we find her. But you stay there instead of here." She held her hands out in a gesture of 'what do you think?' in hopes of getting agreement.

Essie looked at Sharon who seemed as dumbfounded as she felt. Hannah turned slightly toward them and gave them a look. Essie's heart jumped in her chest with the hot prod of hope. Plan B had materialized. If only the captain would agree.

Leaning his head to one side, Captain Fremont looked intently at Hannah. "I know where that is, but there's a fort there. The last time we was there, they tried to incarcerate us. What are ya trying to do? Get us bound in chains for eternity?"

"No!" Hannah said with a tinge of desperation. "That's not our intention at all. The fort closed years ago. No soldiers are there. It's a state park for families and tourists. A place to go for fun."

The ghosts looked dumbfounded. Clem leaned close to Artie and said, "What be a tourist? Ne'er heard of 'em."

Artie nodded and stepped forward to whisper in the captain's ear, "Don't believe her, sir! She be desperate enough to lie to get us out."

"Aye, it's a trick," said Clem. "She lies."

Essie looked at Peg Leg, hoping he'd stand up for Hannah's idea, but he cringed in the corner with Rummy Jones. What a coward! Or did Captain Fremont have a strangle hold on them? Well, the captain didn't have a strangle hold on her.

With anger making her bolder, Essie shook her finger at Clem. "We want you out of here, but we won't lie to do it. The island is a state park, meaning people visit there in the day, and leave at night. We used to go there as girls. The only people in uniform there are the park rangers who take care of the place."

"It's true!" Sharon said, coming up beside Essie. "It's a nice place with buildings and a lighthouse. A perfect place for your kind."

Hannah cocked her head and asked, "Have we done anything to earn your distrust? I haven't called Headless to bring his hellhounds to drive you out. We've allowed you to stay for a little while, but you've overstayed your welcome. It's time to go. Egmont Key is a nice place for you to wait while we look for your lady friend."

"It's the perfect place to wait for Adella!" Sharon sounded eager. Over eager, in fact. Captain Fremont caught on too, as skepticism covered his face.

He stood tall, looking at his dirty fingernails like a man leaving the manicure shop. His lips moved with his inward conversation, but no sound was heard. His crew gathered around him. He put his hands down and stared at Hannah, still seated in the chair. "Me and my boys like it here. Are you girls joining us tonight?" He wagged his eyebrows and held an arm out to Hannah. "We're ready to party."

Hannah hesitated for a moment, then got up and turned her back to him. "At least think about it. I think you'd like it there. Your men would have more room to dance." With a frown and slumped shoulders, she joined her sisters at the door. "Come on, girls, let's go get some rest."

Stepping forward, John stood beside the smug captain. "Captain, sir, beggin' ya pardon." He motioned toward the crew standing across the living room. "Me and the men, we like to dance, but it's pretty crowded here. Mayhap we should have a look-see. Captain. Sir."

Issuing a sound that made Essie's hair stand on end, Captain Fremont faced his first mate.

John held his hands up, pushing back the resentment the captain threw his way. "Captain, we ain't going contrary to ya," John said in a voice of a subservient man. "A better place could be to our advantage." He leaned in close. "These ladies ain't much fun." He gave a wink to the captain.

With the volume of Niagara Falls, Captain Fremont threw his head back in raucous laughter. He took his Superman pose again and told Hannah, "Take one of my crew to this Egmont Key," he said with the tone of someone asking for a ransom. "If he says it's safe, we'll go check it out. I make no promises. If it's not what we want, we stay here."

Essie could hardly control her hopeful fidgeting. If they got the ghosts to agree, the cottage would be theirs again. "I'm sure you'll love it. It's by the ocean. It's lovely and big and private during the nights. It's a wonderful place!"

Not moving, the captain's reddened eyes stared at Essie until sweat broke out on her lip. "Take one of us there. Tonight."

Essie's throat went dry. "Tonight?" she croaked.

Crossing his arms, the captain replied, "Aye. My men want to see it. A reconnaissance trip. See what he thinks."

Panicked, Essie looked at Hannah for help, but got none. "But it's closed this time of night. We can't get in and there's no place to rent a boat to get there. Can't you float to it? We'll give you a map." The captain's burning eyes were hurting hers. She looked away.

"You—" the captain stabbed the air with his gauzy

finger "—will transport my agent there. Take him in that land ship of yours."

Land ship? Essie looked at Hannah.

Coming to her rescue, Hannah said, "One step at a time. We'll take John there in our land ship." She couldn't hide her smile at the term. "But not tonight. Tomorrow. We—" she waved her arms indicating the three sisters, "—can't go to the island, but we'll take him as close as we can. It's up to him to cross over the channel and look around on his own. Agreed?"

"No. It must be tonight." The captain crossed his arms

"I don't know if I can stay up all night," Sharon muttered from behind Hannah.

Hannah waved her sister away. "Why tonight?"

"Because I say it. Agree or we stay."

Essie knelt down beside Hannah and whispered, "I'm too tired to be driving around tonight. Get him to wait until tomorrow."

Rubbing her temples, Hannah shook her head. "We'll stop and get strong coffee or espresso somewhere," Hannah said under her breath. "That should keep us awake. He's offering a thread of hope. Let's grab it." She turned back to the captain. "Agreed. We'll go tonight."

Essie held her breath. She hated the idea of driving around at night with a ghost in the car. Who'd sit in the back seat with him? Not her!

Captain Fremont folded his arms. Essie could almost hear the wheels turning in his mind like a roulette wheel. She wondered where the ball would stop.

The edges of the captain's moustache slowly moved up. "I agree to your terms. Clem—" he motioned to the crewman who called her a liar to step forward— "go with the ladies to see what's at Egmont." He turned back to the sisters and leaned closer to them. "I warn you, if you try to trick me, I won't go easy on you."

Hannah shook her head. "We prefer John. He's your

second, after all."

"You'll take who I say. Clem!"

Clem glided in front of Captain Fremont. Emoting an enthusiastic salute, he shouted, "Aye, sir!"

Captain Fremont put his hand on his sword, either as a threat or as a way of making sure his man understood the seriousness of his assignment. "Go with the ladies to this island. Look around. See what's there. I want to know if what the ladies say is true."

"Aye, sir!" Clem yelled out. The rags he wore flared out as he spun around to look at the sisters. He let out a lecherous chuckle through his snaggle-toothed grin.

Drawing his sword, Captain Fremont placed the blade on Clem's shoulder, with the sharp side up against his neck. "You will treat these ladies like you'd treat my Adella McPhee. Or I'll send you straight to the devil himself. Savvy?"

Clem deflated like a balloon with a slow leak. "Aye, sir," he said in a low tone. He dragged his ghostly feet as he followed Hannah out the door to the land ship.

An hour later, Essie sat in the back seat of the convertible, sipping her keg-sized diet cola while she looked at the crescent moon. Sharon snored softly beside her. The miles seemed interminably long as Hannah drove toward Egmont Key State Park.

Clem sat in front with Hannah as she drove along the highway. He seemed to be having the time of his life aboard the land ship, holding his hands up so the air blew through them. When he tired of doing that, he leaned through the car door to see how close to the fast-moving ground he could come.

Essie hoped he'd blow out along the road somewhere, but the air seemed to pass through him without pushing him out.

After an eternity of time, Hannah turned down the palm-lined road that led to the parking lot for the ferry to the island. The road was completely dark, with only the moon and stars to light the surroundings. Dim lights reflecting on the water were the only indication of where the island was. Pulling into the parking spot closest to the pier, Hannah turned off the car. "This is as far as we can go tonight. The rest of the way is on your own."

Clem sat in the car looking out into the darkness. "It's a long ways over there."

Fatigue from being up after midnight and aggravation of the situation drove Essie to shout, "Not our problem! The captain told you to go check out the island. We brought you this far. The rest is up to you. Go or you'll have Captain Fremont to answer to. And he won't be happy if you don't give him a full report!"

Clem glared at Essie and opened his mouth to speak, but Hannah cut him off. "Get going! We don't have all night!" With a gesture of disgust, the ghost floated through the door and disappeared from sight, leaving the sisters to wait.

Sharon rustled in her seat. Yawning and wiping her eyes, she muttered, "I don't like being out here in the dark. I don't feel safe."

"Me neither," said Essie. She sucked out the last drops of cola from her large cup. "What if we find an all-night restaurant? Coffee would taste good."

Hannah hit the button that brought the roof over them. Locking the doors, she slumped in her seat and put her head back. "Let's sleep. Get comfortable. No telling how long he'll be."

Biting her lip to keep words of frustration back, Essie unclicked her seatbelt and shrunk down on her side of the back seat. No sense wasting energy on this lost battle.

The eastern sky was gray when Clem came back to the car. With a howl, he awoke the sleeping sisters, scaring them out of their wits. He whooshed through the car, in and out and around them.

Essie screamed as Hannah flailed her arms in defense. Sharon curled into a sobbing ball on the back seat.

Essie punched Hannah from behind. "Get us out of here!"

In a flash, Hannah started the car and punched the accelerator, throwing Essie and Sharon against the back. The car fishtailed slightly on the pavement, throwing Essie against Sharon who was still curled on the seat. With a whispered apology, Essie pushed herself to her side of the car again. Her heart pounding in her ears, she clawed around searching for the seatbelt. Finding it, she quickly snapped it around her and pulled it tight.

Clem floated into the front seat beside Hannah as she moved the car back down the long palm-line road. They met a car or two on the way in, likely rangers or ferry workers coming to work. Turning out onto the highway, she turned toward home.

Essie's heart finally settled back into place enough to let her speak. "What did you think?"

Clem let out another howl, causing Essie and Sharon to cover their ears. "Captain Fremont'll be real happy there. Ye'll never guess who was there. Miss Hessie and Miss Etta! Miss Hessie always fancied John. When I tell him where she's at, he be jumpin' ship to get here." Another howl filled the car.

"Shush!" Essie called from the back seat. "Someone will hear you and think we are doing the howling."

Clem let out a laugh. "Let's go tell the cap'n that we're coming to Egmont!"

Hannah sped up.

Essie wiped her weary eyes burning with the need to sleep. She checked to make sure the car was in the correct lane. To her relief, it was so she assumed Hannah was awake and okay with driving. They should arrive back at the cottage by breakfast time. The ghostly ordeal might finally be over.

They could call their mother back to visit. After that, they'd go home. Home. Back to her comfortable bed. Back to her family. Back to normal sleeping patterns. For the first time since she'd arrived in Florida, her body relaxed as she leaned her head in the corner and quickly fell asleep.

"Essie, wake up." Sharon tugged on Essie's arm, pulling her out of her deep slumber. Red lights flashed through her eyelids, causing her to awaken suddenly.

"What's going on?" Essie sat up and looked around.

Behind them was a policeman getting out of his vehicle. His partner walked to the passenger side of the convertible.

Without moving her head, Hannah whispered loudly, "Quick, Clem, disappear!"

Essie's heart was beating so loudly that if anyone else could hear it, it might be interpreted as a dead giveaway something strange was going on. Undeniably, something strange was going on. She and her sisters hauled a pirate ghost to a state park where he found friends. Nothing illegal about that, but it was definitely strange.

She inhaled a ragged breath to calm herself. She heard Sharon's quick breathing next to her. She reached out to squeeze her hand. They didn't need a full-blown anxiety attack.

Clem faded from sight when the policewoman arrived at the passenger door. She signaled for the window to be put down.

Hannah rolled the windows down and turned to the policeman by her window. "Good morning, sir. Have I done something wrong?"

The policewoman shone her flashlight through the car, temporarily blinding Essie with the beam. "I'm Officer Hanover. There were four people in this car when we passed by you. Where's the other person?"

"As you can see, there are only the three of us," Hannah said. "You must have seen a shadow or something."

The officer by the passenger door shown his flashlight through the car again. "We were sure we saw four. Where are you going?"

"We're going home."

"Home from where?" the policeman asked as he

shined his flashlight in the car, blinding Essie again. "Where's home? Seems like I've seen you somewhere before."

Essie looked out her small window, but the shadows were hiding the policeman's face. If the sun were up a little more, she could've seen him. The voices sounded familiar, but where would they have met them? The last time she'd heard that voice was at the cottage—

She looked again. "Is that you, Officer Stanus?"

Officer Stanus quickly shined his flashlight in her face. She squinted and held her hand up to block the bright beam. "Now I remember. We met when you came to our mother's cottage last fall to ask about Howie Howard's visit. Then I visited you the other day about problems with the neighbors. Or I should say their problems with you."

A sharp intake of breath came from the passenger side window. "You're the sisters from the cottage?" the policewoman asked. "The haunted cottage?"

Officer Stanus growled. "This is them. Did you have a ghost in here with you?"

The words froze Essie. How should they answer? Truth, and be thought crazy? Lie, and be thought crazy? If the ends were the same, truth was always best.

"Yes, we are taking a ghostly friend for a ride."

Hannah's head dropped into her hands. Sharon poked her arm and gave her a what-are-you-doing look. The officers stood, probably so they could communicate across the top of the car.

Essie didn't care. Why hide it? As long as Clem stayed invisible, no one could prove her right or wrong. "Officer Stanus, don't you believe in ghosts?" The flashlight beam hit her face again. To save her vision, she put her hand over her eyes.

The officer cleared his throat. "I don't know. Not really, but strange things have happened that I can't explain. But enough of that. What are you ladies doing out here this time of morning? You were weaving in your lane which is why we stopped you. Have you been drinking?"

"Certainly not!" Sharon cried out. "Hannah, if you're tired, you should let Essie or me drive."

"I'm fine," Hannah replied as she looked in the rearview mirror. "I had lots of coffee. I'm wide awake. I was distracted by your snoring."

The officers stood up. Officer Stanus said over the top of the car, "I don't smell alcohol. I think they're clean." Hanover must have agreed because they bent down to look in the windows again. "We still need to see your driver's license and registration."

"Of course," Hannah said, digging through her purse. The glove box popped open and the papers fluttered. "Stop it!" Hannah said under her breath. She reached in and got the rental car papers. The glove box closed by itself. She pulled out her driver's license and gave it to Officer Stanus.

Officer Stanus took the documents and returned to the patrol car to call it in.

"I've never seen a remote-control glove box," Officer Hanover said while her flashlight beam stayed glued on it. "Is that something new?"

Essie's heart nearly stopped, but she found her voice despite it. "You know how these new cars are. They put buttons here and there for everything." She laughed nervously, joined by her sisters.

Officer Hanover shone her flashlight through the car again. "I'm sure we saw four people in here."

Hannah sighed heavily. "We told you we are taking a ghost for a ride."

Essie knew she should support Hannah, but her throat was too dry to allow it. She'd already said enough. Sharon's breathing was rapid, and Essie knew she was about to fall over the edge of panic.

"Is that why you two are sitting in the back seat?" Officer Hanover asked, leaning over. "To make room for your pirate friend?" The cord on her shoulder radio flicked up. She batted at it like it was a fly buzzing around her face.

"I'm surprised one of you isn't up here with your sister while she's driving." The cord flicked up higher and hit her cheek. She looked down and put it back into place.

Hannah sat up a little more. "Pirate friend? Why do you say that?" The cord moved again.

Essie joined in Hannah's glare at the seemingly empty passenger seat.

The cord stopped moving.

Officer Stanus came back with what he'd taken from Hannah. "You're clear to go. Please drive carefully. If you're tired, pull over to sleep or let someone else who's not tired take over."

"Yes, sir." The glove box sprung open by itself again, and Hannah slid the car rental papers back in. She put her driver's license away as the two police officers returned to their car. "Clem, if I could wring your neck, I would."

He let out a laugh, making the police officers pause and look back. Their flashlight beams lit the interior of the car. Hannah reached out and waved her hand at them and rolled the windows up. She put on her blinker as she drove away. Clem reappeared in the passenger seat. Essie slunk down in her seat as far as her seatbelt would let her go. These ghosts were going to get them into trouble yet.

Chapter 9

Sharon

Sharon stretched and yawned in her childhood bed at the cottage. Too tired to change after their all-night trip, she'd kicked off her shoes before pulling the bedspread over her. Her dreams must have been troublesome because her blouse was twisted around her to the point of being uncomfortable.

The faint light coming through the window meant it was either cloudy and rainy or she'd slept the whole day away. She picked up her cell phone from the nightstand and saw it was a little of both. The three o'clock sun was hidden behind rainclouds. Her heavy eyelids gave in to her body's request for more sleep.

A soft knock at the door was followed by Essie asking if she was awake. Her body would have to wait for more sleep. She called out to Essie who came in and sat on the edge of her bed.

As if reading Sharon's mind, Essie said, "I'm still tired too. I desperately need a good night's sleep. I thought I was tired when the triplets kept me up at night, but I think this is worse. This ghost business is too hard on me."

Sharon laughed, her voice still gravelly from sleep. "Me too. I'll be glad when they're living on the island instead of our cottage. Knowing they're in the attic gives me the creeps. It's like we have no privacy at all. And they're an ornery bunch."

Hannah came in, rubbing her eyes. "I thought I heard voices in here." She sat on the bed by Essie. "I want those pirates out of here tonight. But first, we have to figure out how to get that crew out to the island. They won't all fit in the car."

Sharon groaned. Another obstacle to ending this never-ending ordeal. "I still don't know why they can't walk or float or whatever they do, over there. Can we pack them down in the truck? Or they can sit on the hood, as long as they stay invisible?"

Hannah shrugged. "No idea. I've never had to transport ghosts anywhere. I'm still wondering why we have to take them. Why can't they leave the way they came?"

"Because it's part of our agreement!" Captain Fremont floated down through the ceiling. "I trust you ladies are decent." He gave a little growl.

Mad at him for his unannounced appearance, Sharon growled back, "Save yourself for Miss Hessie. How dare you intrude on our conversation without being asked!" She pulled the spread up to her chin.

Captain Fremont shrugged. "We pirates have no manners, do we." He laughed again. "As you were saying, you take us to the island tonight. And no, you can't stuff us in the back of that little car. We expect to be treated like we are regular people, because we once were."

Essie snarled a little. "Pirates are not regular people."

The captain held up his index finger to stop her. "Never ya mind. I expect to be treated like I was alive."

"Whatever," Essie said gruffly.

Hannah cleared her throat. "We can make several trips to haul you all there. Or we could rent a bigger vehicle. A U-Haul truck for example."

Sharon's heart skipped a beat. She hadn't driven a car in nearly twenty years. She'd be no help in this endeavor. "Do you know how to drive a big truck? We've already been stopped once because of your driving."

Hannah huffed. "It wasn't my fault! I wasn't weaving in the lane. It was their imagination. Like seeing four people in the car." A slight smile spread across her face, but it faded. "No, I've never driven anything larger than a minivan."

Sharon rubbed her forehead. Her sleep-deprived brain struggled to focus on a germinating idea, but the pieces hadn't come together yet. A minivan. Or a regular van. She'd seen one somewhere other than the roads. It was parked somewhere. But where? It was here! But whose was it? She softly pounded her forehead with her fist, trying to jar the memory. A van. A black van. The paranormal guys' van!

"That's it!" she shouted.

Hannah and Essie jumped up wide-eyed and dancing around.

"The paranormal guys had a big van! They know how to drive it. They'd help us."

Essie clutched her heart as she sat on the bed again. "What a great idea! We can tell them they can get additional material to study if they drive our guests out to the island. I bet they'd be thrilled to do it."

Hannah was all smiles. Nodding her head, she said, "You've done it again, Sharon. You solved our problem."

Captain Fremont backed up away from them. "Those people who carried those silly instruments and tried to talk to us? Who tried to capture our images on their machines? Never!"

"Oh, don't be so picky," Hannah said as she rose to go. "They'll treat you like humans and take you to see Miss Hessie and Miss Etta. We hear John wants to get there fast." She paused, and half-turned back. "Could it be one of them is his long-lost love?"

The captain let out a rumble. "Her? She ain't nothing special. Loverboy John had a dalliance in every port. If Miss Adella McPhee had been there—" His hand went to his heart, as if her name poked it with a sharp stick "—I would go now." He shook his fist at them. "You promised to find her." He grew bigger. Taller. Enough to fill the room. "Where is she?" he boomed.

Feeling heat emanating from the captain, Sharon's chest tightened, making it hard for her to breathe. They had no defense. They hadn't looked for Adella. They'd left that job to Jeff, Rusty, and Clay. They should have gone to the library and searched for clues. They could at least defend themselves for not having found her yet.

Guilt tightened her chest more, making her breath shallow. One of her hands went to her chest and the other grabbed the edge of the bedspread, bringing it up to shield her from the angry heat. Pulling it over her face blocked the sight of the angry captain.

Hannah met the pirate head-on. "Knock it off! You're scaring my sisters!"

Someone sat on the edge of the bed and patted Sharon's leg. Pulling the cover down low enough to peek over the top, she saw Essie looking at her with a sympathetic eye, and a longing to crawl under the covers to hide with her.

Captain Fremont took on the stare-down with Hannah.

Sharon held her breath as she pulled the bedspread closer to her face. It wouldn't shield her much from whatever might come from their faceoff, but it was all that was within reach. From the corner of her eye, she saw Essie move from the edge of the bed to the wall.

Essie softly cleared her throat and spoke with the voice of a mouse scared to come out of its hole. "We're still looking for her. But someone who has been lost for two hundred years, it's going to take a while to find her. You've waited this long. Surely a few more days won't hurt you."

Sharon pulled the cover down slightly. "When we find her, we'll come to Egmont and tell you. Immediately. As soon as we know, we'll come tell you. Day or night. We promise." She drew an X across her heart and held her hand up.

The pirate turned to stare at Sharon. He crossed his arms and tilted his head to the side.

She held her breath, waiting to see how he would react. He didn't go for his sword to cut out her tongue. Clutching her chest, she hoped with all her panicked self that Captain Fremont would take the offer. If he did, she'd go to the library tomorrow and do research on Miss Adella McPhee. No more waiting on others to do the job for them.

Hannah cocked her head at the shrinking ghost. When he returned to normal size, she asked, "How about it? Will you ride in the van with your men? I'm sure Jeff and his friends would love to take you to the island."

Turning his attention back to Hannah, the captain nodded slightly. "Aye, we'll go. But there be one condition."

Narrow-eyed and smirking, the captain paused long enough for Sharon's heart to stop. She twisted the edge of the bedspread into a tight knot.

"Ya three must go along. If'n I don't like the place, ya bring us back. There'll be no stranding us on a deserted island. I want a proper escort." The captain rocked on his heels as he waited for an answer.

Sharon wrung the bedspread harder. Getting into an already crowded van with ghosts didn't seem like a good idea. There weren't enough seat belts to go around.

She opened her mouth to speak, but Essie interrupted her. "Why do we have to go? The guys know where to go." She peeled herself away from the wall. "Why do you need us? Can't you go there like the way you got here?"

The captain laughed. "Aye, we could, but being a stowaway is not the way I want to go. We came here, riding in big land ships. They sail everywhere, ya know."

Sharon pushed the tightly knotted bedspread away from her. "Getting in a delivery van—um, large land ship, taking you to Egmont shouldn't be a problem. There's no reason for us to go along."

"I want ya there!" The captain grew bigger with anger, and the room grew hot again. "I want ya there!" He settled down a bit. "Or we won't go." He put his hand on his sword and looked from sister to sister.

Hannah threw up her hands. "I'll go in the van with you. Essie, you can drive our car out behind—"

"No!" the captain roared again. "All of ya. In one land ship. There'll be no desertions."

Sharon tried to explain. "It'll be too crowded with three extra people in there. We promise we'll drive closely behind."

The captain held up his hand to stop her. "Ya know my terms. Agree to them, or there's no accord betwixt us." He floated back up through the ceiling, leaving the sisters to agree or not.

Sharon looked at her sisters. Essie was blinking back the tears erupting from her hopeless countenance. Hannah had a black look on her face, like she was ready to kill something. Or someone who was already dead.

The captain was firmly in control of the situation, and he knew it. He'd made his demands. There was little they could do to combat it.

"Let's do it," Sharon said softly so she wouldn't irritate Hannah any more than she already was. "Let's do whatever it takes to get them out of here."

Hannah let out a yes that sounded like a dog's yap before she stomped off to her bedroom. Essie nodded and retreated to her bedroom, leaving Sharon alone in her bedroom. She quickly got dressed and dashed off to the kitchen to see what snacks she could pack for the trip.

Later, Hannah called Jeff on the speaker phone to ask how the data collected during the investigation on their cottage was turning out. Barely able to contain his enthusiasm, he said they had lots of good stuff. They confirmed several ghosts were in the cottage, and they had lots of audio proof, and—"

Hannah displayed no interest in his research. "How'd you like a little more proof?"

"You mean you want us to come out again? I'm not sure our budget will allow us to buy you another hotel room for the night. Your house is very active, and we'd love to spend more time there, but I'm not sure we can afford it."

Sharon heard the disappointment tinged with pleading in his voice. Poor guy. He wanted to prove what they already knew to be true.

"It's not at the cottage we want you to explore," Hannah told him. "It's better than that. It's transporting the ghosts in your van out to Egmont Key." Silence followed her statement. "Did you hear me?"

They heard him cough slightly. "What did you say?"

"We have a vanload of ghosts who want to go to Egmont Key to live. You have a van. How about it? Want to take them?"

"Yeah! When?"

"Tonight. Be here about dark and we'll get loaded up. Set your equipment to run. We may persuade a few of them to make themselves visible to you. We'll introduce you to Captain Fremont."

"We'll be there shortly."

Before the call ended, they heard Jeff in the background let out a whoop. "Come on, boys, we're taking a ride!"

Sharon felt almost as giddy as Jeff had sounded. Tonight, the ghosts would be gone. The cottage would be theirs again! She wanted to dance around, but that could wait until the ghosts were on their way. She felt a strong urge to bake something. Her stomach growled at the thought. "Girls, how long has it been since we had a meal?"

"Too long," said Essie. "Can I help you get supper ready?"

The sun was below the horizon, and the stars were popping out in droves. Sharon sat alone on the porch swing, steeling herself for the time when she'd be stuck in close quarters with ghosts. The thought made her skin crawl and her heart feel like it was going to quit on her. She'd heard of people being literally scared to death. Her fear of the ghosts and her fear of dying blended together to make her heart nearly stop.

In her hand, she held a smooth rock Hannah had given her. A worry stone to squeeze and rub to ease her stress. Its surface heated in her hand with the continuous rubbing, but she couldn't make herself let up. It helped, but it hurt.

A black van made its gravel-crunching way down the long driveway. Jeff, Rusty, and Clay got out and came to the porch where Sharon was waiting for them. She slipped her worry stone into her pocket.

Jeff came bounding up the steps, his eagerness for the adventure barely held in check. "We're here. Are our guests ready?"

Rusty and Clay were close behind with the same excited looks. "The van is gassed up and ready to roll."

"We appreciate your help with this," Sharon said as she signaled for them to sit.

Their eyes kept darting to the door as if watching for someone to come through it.

"Please, sit down. There are a couple of things we must discuss first."

The men complied but fidgeted as they sat there.

Ignoring their restlessness, she went on, "Captain Fremont insists we come with you. That makes three of us, six ghosts, and three of you. Will your van hold that many? Of course, no seatbelts are necessary for the dead."

Jeff gave a quick glance at his van. "We'll make it work. We might have to take equipment out and leave it here though."

Rusty let out a soft moan. He took off his ballcap and wiped his brow. "But we wanted to get additional data while we drove."

Sharon held up her hand. "We know. Trust me, going along is not what we wanted, but Captain Fremont insisted on it. He won't go if we don't. He's a very stubborn ghost."

A flicker of the former excitement filled Rusty's eyes. "We can take our handheld cameras and recorders. We can get good stuff with that. The bigger gear can stay here." They hurried off to prepare the van.

Sharon went inside where her sisters stood with the six ghosts surrounding them. Essie tossed Sharon a sweater. "They're awfully cold to be around. We better be ready for a crowded ride."

The paranormal investigators came in the door. Their eyes widened and mouths dropped right before their equipment dropped from their hands. The ghosts quickly disappeared, leaving behind sounds of surprise, astonishment, and dismay as the men bent down to pick up the electronics on the floor.

"Did you see them?" Rusty yelled out. "Did you see them?"

Clay danced around, pointing at nothing visible.

Jeff let out a hearty roar. "There were bunches of them!"

"And we didn't have our cameras!" Rusty said. He quickly piled their equipment on the sofa and looked around. "Are they still here? Did we scare them away?"

"Pirates don't scare," came the answer out of the air. "Where's the land ship that's taking me to see Miss Hessie?"

Sharon recognized John's voice. No doubt he was ready to go see his girl. Putting her hand in her pocket, she found the worry stone and rubbed it vigorously.

Clay stepped back and held the door open, realizing that was unnecessary. He let it go and ran out to the van.

Jeff went to the door and held it open for the ladies who followed him.

Hannah followed Sharon out. Essie stopped beside him so she could lock the door.

Not eager to be the first in the van, Sharon went out on the porch to wait for Essie. She stopped rubbing her worry stone and let it fall to the bottom of her pocket. A blister was beginning to form on her thumb. The stone wasn't turning out to be as useful as she'd hoped.

Hannah looked inside the vehicle and spoke to the air, "Make yourselves visible. I know you're here."

"Don't trust us?" the captain asked without being seen.

Essie growled to herself, "If she does, I don't."

Slowly, six pirates came into sight, all sitting and leaning on each other in the back of the cargo van, looking like members of a strange rock band. Agog, the three men stared at their passengers. When Clay pulled out his handheld camera, the ghosts faded from sight once again.

Satisfied everyone was there, Hannah motioned for Sharon and Essie to get in.

The cargo van had one seat behind the front seats, normally adequate for hauling three men. Plastic tubs were arranged like pews to provide more seating. There were seatbelts for only three. Sharon felt slightly nauseous at the idea of riding with no seatbelt on, but nothing could be done about it.

Essie climbed in the front door first, going to the seat behind the driver while muttering something about how being the oldest came with privileges. Hannah followed her and sat behind her on a tub. Clay climbed in and sat next to Hannah.

Sharon took the seat by the sliding door. Claustrophobia sat beside Sharon as the door shut with a bang. The top of the tub was springy, and she hoped it would hold her weight without collapsing. Something cold went across the back of her neck and she swatted at it. "Keep your hands to yourself!" she cried out.

Rusty and Jeff climbed in the front. The black land ship roared to life and started down the road. From the passenger seat, Rusty lifted a video recorder facing the back to catch anything paranormal.

Being videoed made Sharon uncomfortable, but she tried not to squirm in her seat. Finding the worry stone in her pocket, her raw thumb hurt as she rubbed it. In the back of the windowless van, the crowded quarters threatened to turn her into a sobbing mess. Her heart beat quickened, and she could feel her breaths coming faster.

Essie leaned over and asked her if she brought a bag to breathe into. Sharon shook her head. In the hubbub to go, she'd left them by her seat on the porch.

She held her hand over her mouth and nose to restrict oxygen. She concentrated on controlling her breathing, ignoring everything else around her.

Road noise in the van was almost deafening. It didn't matter. No one spoke anyway. An occasional cold finger went across her shoulder or the back of her neck. She swatted at whoever was doing it. She saw Hannah do the same thing. Ornery ghosts! Why couldn't they sit still for the ride!

Clay held a voice recorder, hoping to catch something on tape. He jumped when a disembodied voice said, "How much longer do we have to sit back here?"

Jeff yelled from the driver's seat, "About an hour more. We'll be there soon. About midnight." Loud grousing came from the back.

Above the complaints, Jeff said, "Uh oh, we got trouble." He started slowing down and pulled to the side of the road. Flashing red lights lit the ground and the guardrail in front of the van.

Sharon felt her anxiety reach higher levels. She was sitting in a van filled with ghost pirates, on a tub of who knows what with no seatbelt on. No policeman would allow that to continue. She and her sisters would be summarily left on the side of the road. Would the captain and his crew continue on with the three guys or insist on going back to the cottage? The possibilities of bad outcomes seemed endless.

A flashlight beam blinded her. She held her hand up to protect her eyes from the beam. "You again?" Sharon instantly recognized the voice of Officer Stanus. "Still sleeping in the back seat?"

Sharon smiled at the officer and said, "Not tonight. Our driver is taking us to look at the stars. He says there are some pretty spectacular sights in the heavens." As soon as the words left her mouth, she wondered who'd spoken them. Being quick-witted wasn't one of her strengths.

Officer Stanus leaned in and took a whiff. "We've not been drinking," Jeff said. "We're out driving. By the way, why did you stop us?"

Officer Stanus replied, "You have a taillight out." He shined the flashlight through the back seat again. He passed the light by Essie and came back to Sharon. "Is there someone behind you? I thought I saw a face."

Hannah and Clay leaned over and said hello.

The glove box suddenly opened and closed loudly. Startled, Rusty jerked, and Essie let out a small squeal. The officers immediately pointed their flashlights at the sound, but nothing out of place was visible.

Sharon's heart stopped. That crazy Clem! This wasn't the time for pranks. He and his compatriots needed to stay quiet and invisible. If they did, the van could go on its way. Gritting her teeth to keep from expressing her frustration, she longed for the time when they'd get these obnoxious ghosts dropped off and out of their lives.

Officer Stanus waved his flashlight through the van again. "Open the back of the van for us." He motioned for Jeff to get out of the vehicle. On the other side, Officer Hanover asked them to step out.

Sharon's head fell to her chest. The gig was up. They'd be arrested and taken to jail for driving without seatbelts for everyone and for ghosts in the back. How could she tell Santa about what happened? She'd have to call him for money to bail her out. He'd put her on the naughty list for sure.

The door next to Sharon slid open, and she reached for the helping hand to get out. Essie, Hannah, and Clay slid out behind her where they were scolded by Officer Hanover for riding in an unsafe van. Sharon leaned against the van while the officers looked through the back. Vehicles on the road slowed as they went by, no doubt gawking at the scene.

The officers shone their flashlights in and around the back of the van. Peeking around the van door, Jeff gave the group a slight shrug.

"Looks like it's empty back there," Officer Stanus said as he circled his light through the seemingly empty compartment.

"Yes, sir," Jeff replied. "We unloaded the bigger pieces of equipment earlier today. We are taking these ladies with us to look at stars."

Officer Hanover pointed her flashlight in Jeff's face. "What's in the plastic tubs?"

Jeff did a little dance, pushing a few pieces of gravel around with the toe of his shoe. "The tubs are full of cords, radios, and other electronics used during our paranormal investigations. We never know when we'll see something interesting."

"No telescope?" the officer asked. When he waved his hand at an imaginable fly buzzing around his ear, Sharon knew what that signaled. The invisible pranksters couldn't behave when they should. The cord on Officer Hanover's shoulder radio flipped up and she swatted at something touching her arm.

Officer Hanover had had enough. "Something's weird here. These ladies traveling two nights in a row. You ought to be home in bed! You claim to be going to see stars. I don't believe you! I want the truth and I want it now!"

Chapter 10

Hannah

Hannah was at the end of her patience. She hadn't had a good night's sleep since she left home four days ago. Her boys called every day asking when she'd be home. She'd been chewed out for riding in the van. She was watching the pirate ghosts prank the officers. The officer demanded the truth. She'd give it to her.

"We are transporting a vanload of night-howling, furniture-moving, light-blinking, police-pranking ghosts to another location. They won't leave our house unless my sisters and I find a ghost named Adella McPhee, but we can't find her. These ghosts want to visit Egmont Key. We're hauling them out there. These stupid ghosts are the problem. That's why the glove box opens and closes by itself, and flies seem to be buzzing around your ears. It's ghosts who can't keep their mischief in check." She sat down on the ground, crossed her arms, and waited for the inevitable outburst.

Officer Hanover walked over to stand in front of her. She lit Hannah's face with the beam of her light. "You expect us to believe that?"

With a serious chuckle, Officer Stanus told her, "The story is consistent with the history of the calls about their place. I believe it."

Squinting her eyes, Hannah replied, "You asked for the truth, and I gave it to you. We're taking Captain Fremont and his crew to live with Miss Hessie at Egmont Key. His first mate, John, is anxious to get there. Aren't you, John."

A disembodied voice came through the air. "Aye, I am."

The captain showed himself briefly behind Hannah and vanished again. His unexpected appearance triggered a gasp of disbelief from the officers to fill the air. From the space where the specter last appeared came a voice saying, "I don't like constables. Let us be off." A blood-curdling laugh put the exclamation mark on the statement.

The beams of the flashlights shook. "What was that?" Officer Hanover squeaked. She flicked her flashlight through the darkness for the hidden voice. "Who's there?" Seeing nothing, she turned her flashlight on the six people standing and sitting around the van. "Is there someone else with you? Are you playing games with us? We should run you all in."

Hannah was tired of this. "For a missing taillight?" She let out a sigh and hung her head. "We've cooperated in every way. We've told you the truth. We're transporting ghosts to their new home. If you don't believe in ghosts, I can't help you. I can only tell you what I know to be true."

Peg Leg made himself visible before coming over to stand by Hannah. He floated through the van to stand behind her. "Can we go now?" He floated toward the officers, disappearing right before he got to them.

The two officers shuddered as Peg Leg passed close to them. Stunned motionless by what they were seeing, they stood there for a minute, staring ahead into nothing.

Officer Stanus blinked. "Go. Take whatever this is and go. Oh, and fix your taillight." He tugged on the sleeve of his still-paralyzed, bug-eyed partner and hustled back to their patrol car.

"Load up!" Hannah shouted as she went to the van door.

Little was said on the rest of the trip to Egmont Key parking lot. Rustling and soft sounds came from the back, but the living people hardly spoke. Clay held his recorder on his shoulder again, catching anything he could.

Hannah let out a loud sigh as she sat slightly bouncing on the tub. "At least we didn't get a ticket, but don't forget to replace the light bulb."

Jeff snorted. "I'm probably on their watch list of crazy people."

Essie patted him on the shoulder. "But they saw the ghosts with their own eyes. They know we were telling the truth. If you're crazy, they are too. Besides, who'd believe them? It'd make them look silly."

Sharon jumped in. "I bet the police see lots of strange things. Kinda like pilots see UFOs. They'll add their experience to the list of strange stops. Maybe they'll write a book about it someday."

Essie rubbed her temples. "We're back on the road. The sooner we get there, the sooner we can go home."

Hannah nodded. Just like her sister, she wanted this night to end.

Only stars and a slender moon witnessed the van pulling up in the parking lot for the Egmont Key ferry. For a minute, the living ones sat in silence. Jeff broke the spell and opened his door. Rusty jumped out and slid the side door open for everyone to exit the van, including the now-visible pirates.

Rusty had his video recorder pointed toward the ghosts, a huge smile on his face while muttering, "This is so cool!"

Clem pointed toward the small light on the island that marked where the lighthouse stood. "There she be, cap'n. The light house. Miss Hessie and Miss Etta be waiting for John over there." He floated off toward the island without asking permission to leave. "Last one there walks the plank!" he called out as he left. They watched Clem fade into the darkness as he went toward the island.

Even in the dark, Hannah felt her sisters smiling. Her shoulders relaxed as the weight of the last few days lifted. At last! Their unwanted guests were leaving, and peace would return to the cottage. They'd call their mother and father back. She'd go home. Her boys would be happy to know Mrs. Hagg would return to her home. Everything would be back to normal.

One last order of business to conduct. "Before you go," Hannah warned, "remember, this is a place where families go, and weddings are held, and many happy people are around. Don't scare any of them. Behave yourselves!"

A ghostly moan went up. "We not be taking orders from you no more," Artie said.

He and John, Peg Leg and Rummy Jones turned to Captain Fremont. They shuffled around like middle school kids right before the last bell of the day rings.

John saluted his captain. "Cap'n? Permission to go?"

Captain Fremont looked toward the island. He felt inside his shirt and pulled out a woman's necklace from a hidden pocket. He gripped it tightly in his hand as he held it against his chest. "John, you've been a good officer and a good friend. You're in charge of the men. I release you and Artie from your loyalty oaths. Tell Clem I release him too. Go, live with those you find in yon light house."

Artie came to attention beside John who stood motionless. John slowly nodded. "It's been an honor serving with you." He made a slight bow and began to back away.

The captain raised a hand, "Peg Leg and Rummy Jones, yer debt to me remains. Ya will stay with me."

If ghosts could go pale, Peg Leg and Rummy Jones did. They stood frozen to the ground as John and Artie faded off toward the island. Whimpering filled the air. "But, cap'n, sir," Rummy Jones pleaded, "we gave ye a place to stay."

Captain Fremont grabbed the front of Rummy's shirt and pulled him up close to his face. "Yer debt ain't paid yet. A captain needs a crew and someone to run errands for him. That be you two." He released the trembling ghost who shuffled behind his friend. "I will stay on at the cottage until I find Adella McPhee, my true love."

Sharon burst out crying.

The tension immediately came back into Hannah's shoulders. "No, no, no! You're staying here! We found this place for you to wait until we find Adella."

Essie pulled her sobbing sister into a hug, then shouted, "You can go wherever you want to, but you're not coming back with us. You said you'd leave!"

The form of the captain dimmed, but his eyes grew red. "Ya promised to find my Adella McPhee. She's not here. Ergo, ya haven't kept your end of the agreement. I'm not leaving until ya find my true love."

Hannah waved her arm toward Jeff, Rusty, and Clay. "They're looking for her too. Go home with them! They love ghosts. Way more than my poor sisters here."

Jeff kept the camera pointed at the captain. Rusty and Clay took a step back, wide-eyed and stammering something about not finding records of Adella anywhere.

Sharon pushed Essie back. Her hands went together as she begged, "Tomorrow, I'll start looking with them. We'll find her, but won't you stay here until we do? I promise, we'll come get you as soon as we know anything. But pleeease, stay here."

With eyes glowing, Captain Fremont moved toward Sharon. She whimpered and squatted down with her hands over her face.

Hannah quickly put herself between the fuming captain and her kneeling sister. The captain's stubbornness had gone far enough. No one made her sister cry without answering to her for it. Her face felt hot as she snarled, "Enough of this."

Putting out her hand to stop his progress, she told the angry ghost, "You leave her alone. You are not welcome at our cottage. You can either go peaceably to Egmont with your crew or I'm calling Headless to bring his hellhounds to run you off. Either way, you go haunt someplace else."

The captain went face-to-face with Hannah. "I'm not afraid of his hellhounds. I'll not be staying here. I want to keep me eye on you. You'll be keeping yer word."

Hannah never flinched or blinked from the unearthly red glare of his eyes. She stood her ground with her cellphone in hand, ready to call in reinforcements. "Those hounds will tear you to shreds. Plus, you know Headless has connections. You hurt me or my sisters, and Headless will make sure it's the last thing you ever do."

Seconds ticked, measuring the confrontation by molasses drips. The water lapped at the dock as insects sent their chorus into the night sky. Tension gripped the people standing by the van.

Sharon sniffed.

Rusty, holding the camera, moved to get a better view of the infuriated ghost.

Captain Fremont let out a roar and flew at Rusty. The transparent figure flew through the man and disappeared. Rusty fell backwards on the grass like a tree being felled by a lumberjack.

A collective gasp rang out as everyone rushed to him. Circling his prostrate body, they looked down at the man who lay there with a horrified look frozen on his face. Clay knelt beside him and felt for a pulse on his neck.

"Rusty," Jeff whispered, "are you okay?"

Rusty's face twitched a little and the corners of his mouth went up. "Wahoo," he said in a weak voice. "I think that guy went right through me."

Clay took the camera out of the frozen fingers and turned it off. Rusty's fingers moved a little, and he moved his legs. He let out another weak laugh.

"That was a hoot," he whispered as he took Jeff's offered hand and sat up. He felt his chest, his head, arms, and legs. "I seem to be in one piece, but no slime." With help, he stood up again.

Jeff brushed the grass and sand off his back. "What did it feel like?"

Rusty took a shaky step. "Cold and crowded. I think I got everything recorded. By the way, where did he go?"

Hannah pointed at the van. "There. He's going back

with us, and I don't think there's anything I can do about it."
Her legs felt weak. She wanted to join Sharon on the ground
and cry too.

Sharon waved an arm in the air until Essie reached
out to help her up. She dug in her pocket and pulled out a
tissue she used to wipe her face. "Naughty ghost! He has no
qualms about breaking his word."

Essie put her hands on her hips. "He's a pirate. I don't
think they have qualms."

Rusty let out a whoop and danced weakly around the
ladies. "That was the best experience I've ever had! And I've
had a lot of them. Man, ghosts in our van! And it's all on
video. Let's see it!" He bounced and jumped around Clay as
he looked at the video.

Clay wasn't smiling. Hannah knew something wasn't
quite right. "There's nothing but static, or it's too dark to
see."

Rusty ran over and looked at the small screen. His
elation crashed around them. "We got nothing? Their energy
must have interfered with how the camera worked."

Jeff joined them as they looked at what they'd
captured. "When we get it run through filters, something
might be there. Don't give up on it yet." He slapped Rusty on
the back. "You're right, Russ, what incredible personal
experiences we've had. Wow! Never seen anything like this
before." The three men congratulated each other and pumped
their fists in the air.

In the dim light, Hannah saw her sisters looking at
her. Sharon came up and leaned on her. Essie did likewise.
No hand pumping or celebration with them. Three ghosts
were gone. Three were left. She had to find a way to free
Rummy Jones and Peg Leg from the captain. He'd free them
when they found Adella. But where was she? Too much
fatigue made her mind slow. She'd think about it later.

"Gentlemen?" Hannah asked right before she
yawned. "Can you take us home? We've had all the personal
experiences we can endure. It's time for us to rest." She

didn't wait for agreement before climbing into the back of the van. No ghosts could be seen, but she sensed the three of them were there.

Essie let Sharon have her seat, and she crawled in back to sit with Hannah. Sitting on the tubs was uncomfortable without a seat back, but what choice did they have? Hannah leaned against Essie who leaned back against her.

Clay took Sharon's seat so he could talk to Rusty and Jeff as they headed home. The men talked excitedly about the next steps in their investigation as they drove through the dark. Their chattering bored Hannah. She dozed off as they went along. She was awakened as the van slowed and pulled to the shoulder of the road. Flashing lights lit up the night.

Not again! They'd been through this once. How could they get the taillight fixed this time of night? If it was Officers Stanus and Hanover, they'd be through with them in a hurry and send them on their way.

A flashlight beam came inside the van, lighting up the occupants except for the ghosts. Officer Hanover's voice rang through the van. "Get your ghost friends dropped off, did you?"

Hannah, as weary as she'd ever been in her life from past few days and the night rides, groaned out, "All but three." In the spotlight, she shielded her eyes from the pain it caused her.

Unseen, Officer Stanus called from the other side of the van, "We wanted to make sure you ladies weren't dropped off somewhere. We wondered if you were being forced to ride along and dumped out against your will."

Sharon squinted as she said, "That's very thoughtful of you. We're fine and on our way home. Officers, please, we'd like to get there before sunup."

The radio on the officers' shoulders crackled to life, calling for assistance at a domestic disturbance. "Glad to see you ladies are okay," Officer Hanover said as she circled her flashlight beam through the van again. "Have a good rest of your evening." The officers rushed back to their car and left with the lights and siren going.

Jeff laughed. "I guess they thought we were kidnapping you ladies and would abandon you at the light house. Like we'd force you to do something you didn't want to." He started the van and pulled back onto the road.

Hannah readjusted how she was sitting so she could lean against the side of the van. "I'm sure they'll be glad when we get off their road. So, what's next, boys?"

Clay said, "We'll analyze our video and see what's there. After we run it through our filters, we might be able to make out what happened tonight. Then—"

"No!" Sharon cried out from her seat behind the driver. "Forget the video! You have to help us find that lady ghost. Only then can we be rid of Captain Fremont. Don't analyze anything until we find her. We need your undivided attention to this problem. Find Adella, then do your research." Her hands went over her face, and over her mouth and nose. Her panicked breathing was heard through her fingers.

Hannah buried her face in her hands. Would this night ever end?

Chapter 11

Essie

Essie sat quietly on a plastic tub behind Sharon. Reaching around the seat, she patted her sister's arm. Anxiety electrified the air, but there was nothing Essie could do to help. Her own nerves were stretched thin. The slightest prod would push her into her own zone of—what? A nervous breakdown? Insanity?

Essie forced her tight fists to uncoil. Her shaking hands went to the sides of her head to stop her brain from running away to the land of crazy. Her frazzled nerves had had all they could take. She closed her eyes and wished with every fiber of her being to be somewhere else. Anywhere else but here. In a van in a foreign country with her sisters, strange men, and cranky ghosts. Please, please, please, let me be home.

She ran her fingers through her sandy hair. Grit was everywhere around her. In her clothes, her hair, her shoes. A charge of anger expelled her anxiety as she slammed her fist on her thigh. No more. No more sleeping on the beach. With the three noisiest ghosts gone, the cottage might be quiet enough to sleep at night. It was time to reclaim what was theirs.

The whine of the tires drowned out any other sounds. Essie closed her sleep-deprived eyes. The end of this trip couldn't come fast enough to please her. If they didn't get stopped again, they might be back at the cottage soon. Still, the officers had been concerned for their safety. It was comforting to know they were checking on them. Imagine it. Being forced to go somewhere you didn't want to and abandoned by the side of the road. What kind of person would do that?

A thought unexpectedly developed in her head. What kind of person would do that? Someone who hated someone else. Someone who didn't want a person to be found. "Hey!" she yelled out. "Hey, I have an idea!"

She waved her index finger at her van mates. "It hit me when I was thinking about the officers talking to us. They thought you might be forcing us to go with you. That you might have abandoned us somewhere. I have a question for you, Captain Fremont. How sure are you Adella would remain where you told her to be?"

A disembodied voice came from the back of the van. "Adella promised she would wait for me at the White House Inn. She was a woman of honor. She should have been there."

"You said an admiral was mad because you were leaving the service to marry her. What if he forced her to go somewhere so she'd be gone when you got back? What if he thought if you thought she was gone, you'd keep sailing his ships?"

Road noise seemed to grow louder, filling the van until it almost seemed to burst at the seams. Slowly, a low rumble made its way above the noise. The rumble grew until the cry of a broken heart morphed into a roar of unrelenting rage.

Essie covered her ears with her hands as the volume increased. Her hands weren't thick enough to block the screeching. Peeking through scrunched eyes, she saw Clay, Sharon, and Hannah were suffering as much as she was. When the van fishtailed across the highway as Jeff fought to keep it under control, fear pushed a scream out of her. She was going to die!

The loud noise stopped like a switch had been hit, leaving Essie screaming at the top of her lungs. Her voice was not the only one ricocheting off the walls of the van as it bounced off the road and into the grass. The van and the screaming came to an abrupt stop as dust swirled around outside and gear and equipment and people settled toward the front of the van.

Cold air crossed her face as she heard the captain say, "You've hit upon it! Why me true love wasn't at the white house like she promised. The admiral—" He let out the low groan.

"Stop!" Essie yelled at the top of her lungs. "No more groaning! You'll rupture our eardrums if you do it again." Opening her eyes, she saw his face inches from hers in the dim light. She quickly closed her eyes again and willed her racing heart to slow. Her request was ignored.

Hannah came to her rescue. "Captain, how could the admiral have forced her away? People would have seen him. Surely they'd have let it slip what happened."

The cold left Essie's face. She peeked with one eye to see if it was safe to look again. The captain had moved back to the rear of the van. He sat cross-legged on the floor and put his head in his hands.

"The admiral had a strong hold on the town. All feared him. They'd keep his secret under the threat of death."

Sharon stirred from her paralyzed posture. "Sounds like a drug lord."

Captain Fremont tilted his head like a pup. "Some called him a lord, but no one could've drug him anywhere he didn't want to go."

Sharon's eyebrows rose as her voice squeaked out, "Oh, no! You misunderstand. A drug lord—"

Jeff threw the van into reverse and revved the engine. Backing the van onto the road again, he yelled back while looking in the rearview mirror, "We gotta go. I'd hate for the cops to come back and find us here. They might think we're dumping bodies. Hang on!" Throwing his riders back, he spun out on the highway, heading toward the cottage.

The moon hung in the western sky when the sisters made their way up the steps of the cottage. The sound of crunching gravel faded as the van went down the driveway toward the road. The cool ocean breeze rustled the grasses into a soft chorus of sound.

Fatigue from the long night's work weighed on Essie like a lead suit. Sharon fumbled with the key, trying to unlock the door. Hannah grouched at Sharon and grabbed the key out of her hand to try her luck at opening the door. Essie bit her bottom lip, holding back her own impatience.

Out of the corner of her eye, she watched Captain Fremont, Rummy Jones, and Peg Leg float through the cottage wall. Envious of their abilities, she took a step forward to make her attempt to float through the wall when the door gave way. Hannah stepped inside the cottage. Sharon followed close on her heels.

Essie yawned as she walked inside and toward the hallway. "I don't care how many ghosts are in the cottage. I'm sleeping in my bed."

A tall dark figure came out of the hallway. "Where have you been?" a deep male voice asked.

Essie screamed. Her mind went blank, other than sensing her feet wished the rest of her would keep up. Her next coherent thought came when she found herself outside the cottage. She looked around, expecting to see her sisters there with her. A bird's squawk came up from the beach. She was the only one who heard it.

Faint sounds drifted out of the screen door on the porch. Taking slow cautious steps on the porch, she looked inside the cottage. Two figures bent over something on the floor. One stood and turned a lamp on.

Hannah was kneeling beside motionless Sharon, and Headless stood with his hand on the lamp switch.

"Headless!" Essie shouted as she flung the door open and ran to Sharon. "You scared me so bad I nearly pooped a colored egg!" Falling to her knees, she grabbed Sharon's limp hand and patted it hard. "Sharon, are you still with us?"

Hannah patted Sharon's cheeks. "She fainted. That's all."

"That's all! She might have been scared to death. Literally. I know I nearly was."

Sharon moaned and moved her head and arms. Hannah stood up and went to her husband. "How did you get here? Did Santa bring you?"

Headless pulled his wife close and gave her a gentle kiss. He reached inside his shirt and pulled out a necklace. "Mrs. Hagg gave me a talisman that transported me and Shuck here." A large black dog with red eyes came out from behind the sofa and nuzzled Hannah's hand.

Her fight-or-flight adrenaline was urging Essie to run out of the house again, away from the giant devil hound that reminded her of a murderous menace in a Sherlock Holmes book. Only fear of leaving Sharon at the mercy of the giant creature kept her in place.

Hannah sat on the sofa and cuddled the beast like he was the family lap dog. It licked her face while his tail wagged so fast it could hardly be seen.

A sigh of acquiescence expelled itself from Essie's lungs. She gave up. She'd faced ghosts, ridden in a van of strangers, been stopped by the police, forced to sleep on the beach, and searched for the long-lost love of a pirate. How much crazier could it get?

Chapter 12

Sharon

Faint voices came through the fog, but Sharon couldn't understand what was being said. Where was she? She tried to open her eyes, but they wouldn't open. She felt a vibration in her throat and heard a moan. It was her moan. Why was she moaning?

Sharon moved her heavy eyelids. A light was on and somebody's jeans were in front of her face. She closed her eyes again. The back of her head hurt, and she was uncomfortable. Must have been a bad dream. If she was hurt, the dream must be over.

She cracked her eyes open again and tried to focus. A cobweb hung from the living room ceiling, waving at her from above. Time to get up and clean. She moved to get up. Get up? She didn't remember going to bed. No wait. Where she lay was hard and sandy. Why was she on the floor?

The fog in her head was clearing, revealing the memory of a dark figure in the hallway. Her body jerked as she looked around. Her eyes stopped on the huge figure of her brother-in-law standing by the lamp. Headless Horseman! He must have been the dark figures she saw.

Her voice squeaked and broke as she called out, "Tangled balls of lights, Headless! You scared my tinsel stiff!" She tried to sit up, but could only manage to flail her arms and legs.

The tall man's headless body quickly knelt by her

side and helped her reach a sitting position. "I'm sorry, Sharon, I didn't mean to startle you," his head said from the coffee table. "I thought Hannah would be in her room asleep, so I didn't turn any lights on. When I heard a noise out here, I thought it was a prowler who needed to be scared off."

Sharon strained to get to her feet as Headless and Essie pulled on her arms. Her limbs seemed weak and rubbery. Once erect, they helped her to the overstuffed chair. Sinking into its luxurious softness, she patted her still wildly beating heart that seemed to be settling down a little. At least it was still beating.

Hannah held her sides as she laughed. "You scared off one prowler. Did you see Essie fly out the door?"

Essie's legs seemed wobbly as she made her way to the end of the sofa before collapsing. Her face was red as she shouted, "Don't laugh at me. Something dark and ominous came from the hallway. I was scared! You were crazy not to run with me. It could've been the admiral coming to look for Captain Fremont. For revenge or something."

Hannah wiped her eyes. The large hound trotted to her and jumped on the sofa. After a sloppy, wet lick of his jowls, he lay down and put his large head in her lap. He nuzzled her hand, asking for a scratch behind his ears. She scratched him, then told him to get down.

The giant dog obeyed and went over in front of the grandfather clock, circled two times, and lay down. With a giant sigh of a banished pet, he closed his eyes.

Hannah told her sister, "I'm sorry for laughing. I suppose that's a plausible theory. But what I want to know is, what is this talisman, Headless? Mrs. Hagg gave it to you?"

Headless put his head in its cradle on his shoulders. He held out a smooth, black stone with a cord tied through a hole in the middle of it. "Mrs. Hagg gave it to me. I say a few words and zap, here I am. Sweetheart, your calls home were disturbing and left me feeling I needed to come help." He sat on the sofa next to Hannah and put his arm around her.

After a brief snuggle, he rose again, walking in front

of the coffee table where the sisters had their feet propped. "When I get a hold of Captain Fremont, I'll tear him apart! Where is he?"

Three female index fingers pointed to the ceiling.

A snap of his fingers brought the large hound to his side in a flash.

"Fremont!" Headless bellowed. "Get down here! And bring those other—" he seemed to be searching for the right words. He looked at the ladies and pressed his lips together tightly. "Peg Leg and Rummy Jones, you get your sorry carcasses down here!"

The hair on the hound's back stood up, and his eyes grew redder and brighter. The muscles in his back leg quivered, ready to pounce. His teeth peeked out from behind his lips as he started to growl.

Sharon pushed back deeper into the chair. The hound scared her more than the two ghosts descending from the ceiling. Rummy Jones and Peg Leg hadn't bothered her much. Other than being ghosts, they were nice guys.

Reaching the floor, the two ghosts collapsed in front of Headless and clung to each other. Peg Leg was sobbing while Rummy Jones gritted his teeth in a show of strength betrayed by his trembling hands. His eyes were fixed upon the hound who stared back at him.

Rummy Jones looked up at Headless. "I'm sorry, sir. We told 'em not to come, but—"

Headless held up his hand.

Rummy Jones went silent, cowering beside Peg Leg.

Headless walked in a circle, looking up. "I know you're up there, Fremont," he said. "Come down or I'll send my hellhound up and let him drag you down."

Sharon watched the hound, also looking at the ceiling. One front leg raised, it squatted on its trembling hind legs. Given the slightest sign, he appeared ready to spring at the ceiling.

A tense moment passed with no response from the attic. Sharon wondered if the captain had fled the cottage.

He'd gotten here without transport, he must be able to leave without one.

Out of the corner of her eye, she saw Headless flick his wrist. The giant hound took a single leap and passed through the ceiling with a snarl. A shout of pain, some rustling, some growling came right before the hound descended like it was jumping down from the back of a pickup truck. In his mouth, was the leg of Captain Fremont. The dog drug the ghost to the feet of Headless and dropped him.

"Let go of me, you mangy hound!" Captain Fremont shook his fist at Headless. "You have no cause to treat me like that!"

Headless grabbed the pirate by the front of his coat and lifted him up close to his face. "My wife asked you to leave and you refused. You should have obeyed her. I'm here to see you get out of here. No arguments. No excuses. Go before I let Shuck haul you to the devil himself."

Getting quickly to his feet, the captain straightened his coat. "Did she tell you she is helping me find Adella McPhee, my true love? She made an accord with me to find her. Do you want her to break her word?"

The fierce, dark eyes of Headless eased enough that Sharon wondered if he was going to concede the point.

Hannah rose from her seat to stand beside her husband. "I made an accord to help you find her. I've fulfilled my end of that. We've tried. We got experts to help us. We found a home for your crew. Your own obstinance is why you're still here."

"But ye haven't found my Adella!"

"That wasn't part of our deal!"

"Aye, it was!"

The argument went on, becoming louder with each retort. Essie put her hands over her ears and doubled over on the sofa.

Sharon agreed with Essie. The fatigue of staying awake for so many hours rubbed on her body like sandpaper.

Her eyes burned from lack of sleep, and her mind was turning to mush. The argument could go on all night long, but they'd do it without her.

"Captain," she said loudly, "I was there when the accord was made. We agreed to help you look for Adella. We did that. We couldn't find her. We've did our part. Don't be naughty about it. Go your way."

Essie supported her sisters. "As my sisters have said, we've fulfilled our end of the bargain. It's time for you to do the same. We can take you to the island to join your men, but that's as far as we'll go with this. It's time for you to go." She rubbed her eyes and yawned.

Sharon knew how she felt. Her eyelids were heavier than ever. She didn't have the strength to hold them up anymore. "Now if everyone will excuse me, I'll go to sleep now."

She flipped the footrest up on the overstuffed chair, leaned to one side, and was asleep before anyone could protest.

Chapter 13

Hannah

Sunlight filled Hannah's bedroom as she slowly woke out of a deep slumber. Pulling the pillow out from under her head, she rolled over and put it on top of her face. She didn't care what time it was. Her body still craved sleep, and she'd give in to its desires.

Her dreams began again, taking her away to other places and scenes. Scenes of home and her boys with their horses. The pastoral scenes were accompanied by the sound of a phone ringing incessantly. Huntley had a phone. It was probably his. Why didn't he answer it? The ringing was annoying. Someone should answer that phone!

Her head popped up, knocking the pillow to the side. The dream ended, but not the ringing. Her phone on the nightstand beside the bed rang again, drawing her farther out of dreamland and back to reality.

This call had better be good. If it's the boys, blood or fever better be a part of the disruption or her eruption on them would not be pleasant. If it was that Estelle woman, she'd hang up. Anyone else, she might listen.

Her voice scratched out. "Hello?" She cleared her throat and said it again.

"Hannah, we have exciting news!"

The voice was male and young, but it didn't sound like one of her boys. Who else would be calling?

"Did you hear me?" the voice asked. "We think we've found Adella McPhee!"

Hannah sat up, knocking her pillow on the floor. "What? You found her?" She threw off her light covers and ran to the closet to look for her robe. Her brain was clearing. Clay was telling her the news she wanted to hear more than anything. "Where?"

"At the Pensacola lighthouse. At least we think it might be her. The place is reported to be haunted by an angry female ghost. A former lighthouse keeper hated her husband so much she killed him."

"What makes you think it's Adella?"

"I've thought about it, and I think Essie may have been on the right track. Adella wasn't where she promised to meet Captain Fremont. Maybe she was forced to leave. Maybe she was forced to marry someone who would take her away. If you were forced to leave your lover and marry another, wouldn't you be angry? It's worth checking out."

Putting on her black, silky robe, she went into the kitchen where Headless was talking with Sharon while breakfast was being prepared. She waved one hand wildly while the other held the cell phone tight against her ear. "It's a possibility, I guess. When can we find out for sure?"

Holding the phone away from her mouth, she shouted, "Get me a map of Florida!"

Headless and Sharon exchanged puzzled looks. Sharon ran into the other room to rummage through a drawer. Headless stood beside Hannah, putting his arm around her with a quizzical look on his face, but he said nothing. Essie came into the kitchen in her robe asking for coffee. Her half-open eyes were an indication of her half-wakefulness. Rubbing her eyes and yawning, she asked what was going on.

Hannah put the phone on speaker. "How did you discover she might be there?"

The guys must have had their phone on speaker too because Rusty spoke next. "It took a little research. For years, I'd heard about that lighthouse being haunted, but I didn't think much of it because it's out of our normal territory. This morning, we were talking about your situation, and I suddenly remembered it. I made a few phone calls and searched the internet. From what one of my buddies described, the ghost there fits the bill."

Sharon came back in the kitchen with a map and started spreading it out on the kitchen table. "What's going on?"

Hannah grabbed her by the shoulders and hugged her. "The guys think they know where Adella is! She's in Pensacola!"

Squeals of delight echoed through the kitchen as the sisters bounced up and down with joy. Headless stood by the eating bar and smiled at the display of elation. Shuck let out a howl and danced around the ladies.

Essie went to the map. "Where's Pensacola?" She ran her finger around the map searching. "Can we go there today?"

Clay let out a cynical chuckle. "Today? I don't think so. It's like a ten-or-twelve-hour long drive to get there. It'll be a while before we can go. Some of us have day jobs. No offense, but I like to spend my vacation time with my wife and kids."

The balloon of their happiness sprang a leak and deflated. Hannah looked at the map. As the broom flies, it was a long trip over the Gulf of Mexico. Essie traced the car route from Sarasota to Pensacola. The bend in the state made it miles and miles longer. In Santa's sleigh, it'd take no time at all, but the moon was waxing. That option was off the table.

Hannah retrieved her cell phone and thanked the men for their help before hanging up. They were on their own.

Shuck's ears stood up and he growled at something in the doorway of the kitchen. Headless stood with feet apart and arms crossed. "Captain, show yourself."

A stooped form slowly became visible in the

doorway. Peg Leg had his hat in his trembling hands. "Mr. Horseman, sir. The captain, he left last night."

"He's gone?" Hannah asked, slamming her hand down on the countertop. "Now that we need him here, he's gone. Where'd he go? Do you know?"

The ghost toyed with his hat, never looking at her. When Shuck let out a huff, Peg Leg jerked and stammered, "He went to the neighbor's house. You know, the one who came here one day. The one that brought the constable with her? He figured he'd be safe there. He aims to come back here after you ladies go away."

The warmth drained from Hannah's face. Poor Estelle! Her house was haunted by the one she'd complained about. Captain Fremont would repay her for bringing the sisters back to the cottage and disturbing his peace. They had to get him out of there. Fast.

Headless knelt beside his hellhound. "If we get Shuck in the house, he'll drag the scoundrel out of there."

Hannah shook her head. There had to be another way. Estelle might be an overbearing neighbor, but she didn't deserve to be terrified by an unfeeling ghost. "Sharon," she said, "got any of your good coffee cake? It's time we paid a visit to our neighbor."

Neatly cut coffee-cake squares sat on the plastic-wrapped plate Essie held as Hannah rang the doorbell. After a short wait, a man in Bermuda shorts and a striped polo shirt answered the door.

"Yes?"

Hannah put on her sweetest smile. "Hello, we're your neighbors from the blinking lights house. Since we got off to such a shaky start, we thought it would be nice to pay a little visit. We've brought coffee cake for all of us so we can get better acquainted. May we come in?"

The man looked behind him, then back at the ladies. His mouth smiled, but his eyes did not. "My wife is still in her robe. Could you come back in a little bit?"

Unwilling to be put off, Hannah took a step forward,

causing the man to back up. She took advantage of his retreat to take another step and was soon inside the door. "We'll wait. Tell her we're here. Thanks."

The man stammered several times before turning to go find his wife.

Hannah motioned for Essie to come in. Shutting the door behind them, they crept into the living room of the townhouse. Large windows looked out at their mother's cottage and out at the ocean. Lights blinking in the cottage would certainly be disturbing. Hannah understood why Estelle had been insistent about getting it stopped.

Somehow, they had to get Captain Fremont to come back with them. The sooner they got him out of there, the sooner they could see if they'd truly found Adella. Plus, peace would return to Estelle's view of the ocean.

The sounds of muffled arguing came from another room. The sisters' presence wasn't welcome. Estelle couldn't be seen without doing her hair and makeup, and her husband arguing he didn't want to entertain two ladies that long. Too bad they couldn't know why the visit was imperative.

Their argument made Hannah's impatience flair. Truth be known, she didn't need Estelle or her husband to complete her task. "Captain Fremont!" she whispered loudly. "I need to talk to you. We may have found Adella. Do you hear? We may have found her."

The only sounds in the room came from a whirring refrigerator and the backroom argument.

"Captain! Come back. We need you, so we can go see if it's her. We can't know for sure without you."

Essie looked around. "He's not here. Or he's not listening."

Hannah put her hands on her hips. She didn't want to bring Shuck over here, but if she had to, she would. She stood perfectly still. She sensed he was somewhere close. "If you heard us, give us a sign."

A force came down on the plate of coffee cake nearly knocking it out of Essie's hands. She juggled the plate a little before finally getting a firm hold on it. The neatly cut pieces were smashed.

Taking the plate from Essie, she whispered into the air, "Get yourself back to the cottage. We'll take you to the lighthouse where Adella may be." Her hair moved in a cold breeze. "Leave the plate, Essie. Let's go."

"But we can't leave. What will they think?"

"Who cares. We got what we came for." She grabbed the plate of smashed coffee cake and threw it on the sofa. Grabbing Essie's sleeve, she pulled her to the door and left.

The transparent form of Captain Fremont stood in the kitchen of the cottage when Hannah and Essie got back. The captain's eyes were fixed on the hound who returned his stare. Sharon and Headless sat at the kitchen table talking. Peg Leg and Rummy Jones kept a safe distance between them and Shuck.

Sharon took a sip of coffee. "You weren't gone long. How was your visit?"

Essie got two more coffee mugs and poured a cup for her and Hannah. "We didn't visit. Estelle wasn't dressed yet, and we didn't wait for her. No sense in it since we got what we went for."

Taking a mug of coffee, Hannah went to stand behind Headless. "We may know where Adella is."

The captain's eye immediately brightened, and a change in his appearance was apparent. "You...you found her?" His voice was as soft and hopeful as a boy who's asking if he can keep the stray puppy.

Putting a piece of coffee cake on a plate, Essie replied, "Maybe, but not for sure. The ghost guys gave us a good lead. She may be at a lighthouse very far away."

Captain Fremont let out a roar, causing the hound to bark furiously at him. "That scummy admiral! He took my true love from me. Sent her away, he did. Far enough away he thought I'd never find her. May his soul rot in hell!"

Stroking the head of Shuck, Hannah got him to be quiet. "No use having a fit about it. If Adella McPhee is living in the lighthouse, you'll have beaten the admiral. You can live happily ever after with her."

The ghost gave the grin of revenge. "I'll be the one that wins this time. That rapscallion can't keep us apart. Let's be off!"

Sharon let out a loud sigh. "It's a long drive. It'll take all day to get there."

Headless patted his jacket pocket. "Leave that to me."

Still tired from their nights of escapades, the sisters slept most of that morning. Their sleep was a sound one with Headless keeping watch and keeping the impatient captain quiet. He didn't need sleep like his human wife and sisters-in-law did. Wherever his wife's well-being was concerned, he made sure she got her sleep.

Headless also took Estelle's phone call and blamed their hasty departure on an unexpected phone call. He gave an unfelt apology for the inconvenience and promised they'd call before coming the next time.

The afternoon sun was hot when Hannah took her iced tea out on the porch where Headless was sitting on the swing. His arms embraced her as she leaned against him. She felt much lighter. The weight of Captain Fremont and his problems was off her shoulders, letting her relax.

Inside the cottage, her sisters were talking with a generous sprinkling of giggles. Sounds of family. Hannah missed her boys and wondered what Huntley and Horace were doing. Even from here, she knew they weren't happy. She'd have to do something special for them to make up for their time alone with Mrs. Hagg. She'd also have to do something extra special for Mrs. Hagg for giving her Headless a way to come here to her.

Until then, she'd enjoy her quiet time with Headless. She pulled his head off its cradle and kissed him with all the passion her lips could hold.

Chapter 14

Essie

The surf provided the background music for the chorus of crickets and bugs in the sea grass in front of the cottage. The sun touched the water on the horizon, coloring the clouds pink and orange. The water borrowed the palette in its ripples and waves. The pastoral scene would have been perfect, except for the heavy footsteps of a pacing ghost captain ringing out, interjected occasionally with a howl of impatience.

The ocean breeze stirred Essie's black-and-red tunic over her white capris and made her hair brush across her face as she sat in a wicker chair on the porch. Sharon's dinner was settling in her stomach, making her eyes droop even though she'd slept most of the day.

Hannah leaned against Headless on the porch swing as they rocked gently. Shuck slept on the porch step, letting out an occasional snore.

As much as Essie hated to admit it, the presence of Headless was comforting. He was good at dealing with ghosts, and he could have that responsibility. Her head dropped as she rubbed the last of her tension out of her forehead. This visit had been an ordeal, but the end was in sight.

Sharon hurried outside after cleaning the kitchen alone, at her own insistence. She carried a plate of cookies and offered them around. She took two for herself as she sat in the wicker chair beside Essie. "The captain is in a foul mood. He wants to go to Pensacola now."

Headless waved away a fly. "You know, Sharon, I'm amazed at how well you've adapted to being around ghosts. You were inside alone with Fremont and weren't using a bag to breathe into. I applaud your courage."

Sharon let out a huff. "Just because I'm around ghosts doesn't mean I like them. I still prefer living people to dead ones."

Essie agreed. "I'm with you on that. Let's talk about Pensacola. What's the plan? I assume we're waiting until after dark."

Captain Fremont drifted through the wall, followed closely by Peg Leg and Rummy Jones. The two were close behind him. They seemed more afraid of him since the departure of the rest of his crew. Essie suspected the captain's hold on them was a strong one.

Shuck jumped up. The hair on his back stood up as he stared at his quarry. Headless snapped his fingers, and the hound trotted to the side of the swing.

Ignoring them, Hannah explained, "Headless did some research and found the lighthouse is on an active military base. We can't go busting in there at night without getting caught. They likely have security cameras all over the place."

The captain drifted into the middle of them, stood tall, and crossed his arms. "I can get in."

"Then go!" Sharon shouted. "You've overstayed your welcome here!" She squirmed in her seat as she looked at her sisters for support.

Headless held his hands up to restore calm before the storm raged too wildly. "We'll get to that. The ghost at the lighthouse is indeed female, but her name is Michaela, not Adella."

The captain started to protest, but Headless calmed him again. "That's what the internet says. That's not to say if Adella was forced to leave here and that her name wasn't also changed, although that seems like an over-drastic measure."

Essie agreed, but another thought nagged at her. "The admiral may have been double covering his tracks."

The captain started pacing again, the porch vibrating with each step. He stopped in front of Headless, but the porch still vibrated. "The admiral was an evil man. He would have done such a thing."

Headless continued. "Nevertheless, this Michaela was not a happy woman and stabbed her husband to death. She ran the lighthouse after that. It's her, they say, who haunts the place."

Captain Fremont crossed his arms as he let out a chortle. "Sounds like me Adella. She twasn't a lass you wanted to tangle with. She could hold her own in a fight."

Essie's mental picture of Adella changed. She wasn't a petite, fragile girl waiting for her true love on the dock every day. She'd been a tough lady, expecting others to uphold their promises to her. Her fingers curled.

Headless pointed at the captain as he spoke, "There's no guarantee it's her. Before we go to the trouble to find out if it is or not, I want another accord with you." He stood and leaned into the captain's face. "This is the last attempt to find Adella we will make. Whether it's her or not, you will stay there or move on to wherever you want, but you will not return here. Ever. You will release Peg Leg and Rummy Jones from your servitude. Their debt has been paid." He glared at the captain who returned his stare. "Agreed?"

The standoff emitted an unnatural heat, causing Essie's face to break out in a sweat. She dared not brush it away for fear lightning might strike her. She stared at the two men as their resolves battled.

Shuck came up beside Headless. He looked up at the ghost with bright red eyes and a snarl that made Essie's blood run cold.

The skin around the ghost's eyes relaxed slightly and his eyes went to the hound, whose teeth were bared. He took a step back and stuck out his hand. "Agreed."

After his handshake with Headless, the captain called for Peg Leg and Rummy Jones. The two ghosts appeared outside the front door. Captain Fremont walked over to them and spoke in their faces. "You're free to go, you two worthless dogs. But stay away from my treasure, or I'll drag you to hell myself."

Rummy Jones stood tall and saluted the captain, barely suppressing a grin.

Peg Leg stared at the captain and replied, "Aye, sir."

With that, the captain disappeared.

Kneeling before Headless, the two ghosts thanked him profusely for their freedom. Headless dismissed them with a wave of his hand and a reminder to stay out of trouble. The ghosts disappeared in a rush of wind.

Essie felt better. Only one ghost left.

The next afternoon, four people stood in a circle in the living room, along with the transparent figure of their unwanted guest. The plan was formulated, along with a Plan B and an escape plan in case something went wrong. Essie had insisted on it. She was one of the two people going.

Her heart was pounding so hard it was shaking her whole body. Her face was moist, but not from the heat, but fear. Paralyzing fear. Headless couldn't go. He was sending Hannah in his place. She was confident in completing their mission.

Essie was selected to go. Not because she was courageous, but because she didn't get sick on roller coasters like Sharon did. All due to their mode of transportation.

Hannah held the black stone in her hand and asked, "How does this work?"

Headless shrugged, making his head rock a little on its cradle. "I don't know how it works exactly, but it must open a wormhole or something like that. You say the words Mrs. Hagg told me to say. A big squeeze, a little spin, and voilà, you're where you want to go. Quick as that."

Captain Fremont roared, "Leave it to a witch to make

things simple. Traveling this way sounds a mite better than those crazy land ships around here."

Hannah shushed the captain and asked, "What are the words?"

Headless got a quirky smile on his face. "Everyone traveling should hang on to the talisman, then say these words: Pop my bubble, I'm in trouble, take me there on the double. Then say the name of the place you want to go." He looked at Hannah and laughed. "I didn't invent it. She did."

Hannah laughed, and Sharon joined in.

Essie couldn't help but roll her eyes. Nothing seemed funny about it. How could this possibly work?

Even though Essie's stomach was full of butterflies, birds, and a myriad of other things with wings, the words elicited a laugh from her. They somehow made the crazy situation a little easier to handle. How bad could it be? Headless got here in once piece, even with a detached head. She stuck out her hand and grabbed the cord with a stone on it. Captain Fremont did the same, chilling her hand.

Closing her eyes tightly, she waited for something to happen.

"Good luck, honey," she heard Headless say, followed by a smack.

Hannah repeated the words, and said, "Pensacola lighthouse."

Essie felt her body being squeezed into a girdle. A too small girdle. Her lungs couldn't move to suck in air. She felt herself spinning around. She dared not open her eyes for fear of getting dizzy. Her hair blew around her face in the wind blowing from every direction at once. When she thought she couldn't hang on anymore, the wind died, and the girdle began to loosen. She felt something firm under her feet as her head began to clear.

Released from the girdle's firm grip, Essie sucked in a deep breath. Her eyes felt like they were still spinning in her head, causing her to teeter. She felt a cold hand grab her upper arm. The shock of being steadied by a ghost shocked her brain back into stability.

"Got your land legs back?"

She opened her eyes a little and saw a faint Captain Fremont bending over to look at her, his hand on her arm. She nodded and pulled her arm out of his hand. He laughed and faded from sight.

Trees surrounded the small clearing where Hannah and Essie had landed. A sandy path beyond the trees went through a lawn area. Above the trees, the top of the lighthouse shone in the afternoon light. Excitement and hope welled up in her heart and her eyes. Whether the ghost here was Adella or not, the nightmare would end.

Hannah put the talisman in her pocket and went toward the sunlit path. Before emerging from the shadows of the trees, she looked around to see if anyone was watching.

The sisters moved out to the sidewalk where only three other people were walking. Hannah led the way to a bench near the lighthouse. "There you go, Captain Fremont. Go find this Michaela. If she's not Adella, maybe she'll know where she is. Good luck with that. We'll be on our way." She took a step back.

Captain Fremont's voice came out of the air. "Ye can't go yet, missy. Don't ye want to know if it's her or not?"

Essie looked at Hannah and knew she was struggling with the same issue. Curiosity was too strong to resist. They had invested too much time to walk away. They had to know whether Adella McPhee was here or not.

Essie checked her phone for the time. "You have one hour."

Hannah added, "Remember your agreement with Headless. This is the end of the line as far as we're concerned. Whether she's here or not, you're staying."

"Aye. I'll keep my word on it."

They listened closely, wondering if he'd left or not. No matter. Everything was up to him.

Essie looked around at the buildings. "Want to go through the museum?"

Hannah shook her head. "It's a nice day. Let's walk around."

Conceding, Essie followed her sister toward the lighthouse. She pulled out her cell phone and checked the time again. She wished she'd have told the captain to take thirty minutes.

The hour dragged on as they walked along the paths around the site. They returned to the bench and sat, marking each passing minute. Thirty minutes passed. Forty minutes. Forty-five minutes.

With ten minutes left, they heard a voice out of the air behind them. "Ladies, come meet Adella McPhee, my heart's true love."

Chapter 15

Sharon

The afternoon was filled with therapy for Sharon. Inside the cottage wafted the aroma of cookies and bread. Occasionally, the sound of humming added to the cheerful atmosphere. The dining table was set for six.

Headless sat on the sofa watching TV and checking his watch every five minutes. He went through the channels, not staying on one long enough to get involved. His foot jiggled in a nervous way, exposing his fretting over what was going on at the lighthouse. Shuck lay on the sofa beside him, sound asleep.

With the ghosts gone, the cottage was a safe and quiet place again. She didn't mind Peg Leg and Rummy Jones being there. For ghosts, they were nice, and they shared a kinship with their common distaste of the captain.

A warm feeling surged through her when she peeked out at the pacing Headless. His hard bargaining had returned peace and tranquility to the cottage. All those years she'd thought of him as a creepy bloke, true to his reputation. But he'd turned out to be a kind man who loved his family. She'd been too quick to judge.

She cut up the ingredients for salad going with the lasagna she'd made for dinner. When Jeff had called to ask if the captain had made it to Pensacola, she'd invited the three men over to eat with them. Their curiosity was as great as hers. But first, Hannah and Essie needed to get back. How much longer was it going to take?

As if reading her thoughts, Headless came into the kitchen. "I wonder what's keeping them." He checked his watch again. "All they needed to do was drop him off and come back. It shouldn't take this long."

Sharon dried her hands on a towel. "They'd call if there was trouble. Knowing my sisters, they'll hang around long enough to find out if Adella was there or not. The ghosting guys aren't due here for another hour. I expect they'll be back before then." She picked up a bag of freshly baked cookies and handed it to Headless. "When you go back, take this bag of cookies I baked for your boys."

Headless smiled. "Could you throw in a couple extra for Mrs. Hagg?"

Sharon giggled as she opened the bag and added several more cookies. "I love it when people love my cookies. Makes me feel—"

A snap came from the living room. Sharon had heard that sound once before, when Hannah and Essie left with the captain to go to the lighthouse. The snap signaled the talisman's magic had worked again.

Shuck started barking, and Headless spun around to look. His head teetered, and he quickly grabbed it before it fell. He shushed the dog and rushed into the living room.

Sharon quickly followed Headless. In front of the grandfather clock, her sisters stood with their hair mussed and their clothes wound around them. Both had a hand on the chain with the black stone.

"Hannah!" Headless cried out. "I was starting to get worried."

Hannah smoothed her hair and straightened her clothes. "The captain asked us to wait to see what happened. I'm glad he did. I'd have been curious if we'd dropped him off and left without knowing for sure."

Sharon's excitement kept her bouncing on her feet. She had to know. Was it finally over? "Well?" she asked.

A broad grin spread across Essie's and Hannah's faces. "It was her! She's been at that lighthouse since she died."

Sharon let out a whoop and danced around the living room. She grabbed her sisters' arms and they danced in a circle, with Headless laughing as he looked on. "Come join us in our victory dance!" she cried out, breaking the chain and holding her hand out.

Headless declined. "I lose my head when I dance. It's best for me to watch."

Sharon was feeling happy. Nothing could bring her down. "Throw it on the sofa and join in!"

Headless let out a hearty laugh and moved away.

The sisters danced until Sharon was out of breath and had to quit. She fell into the overstuffed chair and put her feet on the coffee table. "The house is ours again! We can sleep in our beds. And we can call Mother back!" She clapped her hands. "But first, supper!"

"But first," Headless said, "I need to get home. The boys have probably reached the limit of their niceness. And Mrs. Hagg will be happy to go home."

Sharon and Essie bid him good-bye and made sure he had the bag of cookies. They went in the kitchen to give the other two their privacy. Sharon put the lasagna in the oven and started the yeast rolls. Essie sat at the eating bar telling her about the sensations of talisman travel. They heard a snap before Hannah came into the kitchen.

Sniffing the air, Hannah said, "The kitchen smells delicious." She rubbed her stomach as she sat down. "I told Headless we'd call him when we're ready to go home. He'll bring the talisman. We can use it to go home. That way we won't bother Santa again."

Sharon carried her dirty dishes to the sink and started washing them. "That's very thoughtful. Santa will be happy to hear it. He said NORAD is tired of clearing him for these extra trips. But I wonder if I'll be able to do it. Does it make you very dizzy? I'm not sure I can handle it."

Essie picked up a towel to dry the clean dishes. "Nothing a little Dramamine wouldn't cure."

An hour later, the black van rolled up at the peak of aromas in the kitchen. Fresh bread, lasagna, and brownies. Jeff, Rusty, and Clay ate until their bellies were filled to the top. Hannah and Essie regaled them with how Captain Fremont had found his true love at last. And how quiet returned to their mother's cottage by the sea.

After the men left and the kitchen was clean, Essie carried a platter of brownies to the porch. Hannah sat in the big wicker chair. Sharon followed with glasses of warm milk. The three of them sat quietly in their seats, watching the ocean and listening to the roar of the surf and sounds of birds. The sun made its way closer to the water.

"We're calling Mother tomorrow, right?" Hannah asked finally. "I'm tired today I wouldn't enjoy it if we called her tonight. Even though I'm starting to get used to staying up all night, I don't want to make a habit of it."

Essie nodded her head. "I agree. As much as I want to go home, I'd enjoy a visit with her more after another night's rest."

Happy to know they were thinking the same thing, Sharon added, "Tomorrow is fine with me. This whole vacation has been nothing but drama. Now that we're rid of our unwanted houseguests, let's take the rest of the day to relax."

Hannah hummed her agreement. "I'd love to spend some time in the ocean. It's calling my name."

Essie asked, "Do you think it's safe to leave the house? There are ghosts out there who know about our place and might want to come back. I'd hate to go through this again."

Sharon groaned. "I hope to never see another ghost again. I've been thinking we should take some of Mother's money and put in a burglar alarm. Let the sheriff deal with prowlers if they come around."

The sisters hummed their concurrence.

The sisters sat and passed the time with small talk and silent mulling until they saw a patrol car coming down their driveway. "Uh oh," said Sharon. "I wonder if we're in trouble again."

They watched as Officers Stanus and Hanover got out. They scanned the surroundings before leaving their car, as if expecting an ambush. Essie waved at them and motioned them to come over. The pair made their way up the sidewalk. Officer Stanus had his hands on his belt and Officer Hanover had one hand on her belt and one on her pistol.

"Good evening!" Hannah called out. "Come join us on the porch! Can we get you coffee or anything?"

"No, thank you. Mind if we sit for a few minutes?"

Hannah got out of the wicker chair and joined her sisters on the porch swing. The two officers sat down in the wicker chairs but didn't say anything. The awkward silence held handwringing and foot twitching.

Hannah tried to put them at ease. "Are you here about that night?"

The officers nodded.

"It was pretty strange, wasn't it."

The officers nodded again.

"Let me reassure you that what you saw was real. Ghosts are real, and you had a paranormal experience with them."

Officer Stanus took off his hat and ran his fingers through his hair. "We weren't sure how to write up the report on the stop. Strangest thing I've ever seen." He motioned toward the cottage. "Your neighbors were right when they said this place was haunted. You keep lots of ghosts here?"

Essie and Sharon laughed. "No!" Sharon said, "We got rid of them last night and hope to never see them or their kind again. It's unnerving to have them around. We prefer our privacy."

Essie concurred with Sharon. "Good riddance to them. We hope they'll be happy out at Egmont Key."

Officer Stanus rubbed his hands together. "Um, that's what we're here about. There's no law against it, but what's with taking them there? It's like illegal dumping in a state park in a way, but we can't prove anything. Maybe there should be a law against moving ghosts to a public facility."

Hannah sat up. "Like you said, since there's no law against paranormal dumping, we're not guilty of anything. Besides, there were already ghosts out there. Lady ghosts."

"How do you know that?"

"Our ghosts told us," Sharon said. She held out her hand, palms up, to the stunned officer as if to say, 'the truth can be strange.' "We had no reason to doubt them. They seemed anxious to get there to see friends."

"By the way," Essie interrupted, "we won't be driving around at night anymore. If you need us, we'll be right here in our own beds."

"That's good news," Officer Hanover said as she rose to go. "I'm not sure I could handle another stop like that one." They shook hands with the ladies and bid them good day. The sisters watched as they left in their car.

Sharon laughed a little. "I feel a little sorry for them. I was shocked when I first saw Peg Leg and Rummy Jones. If you hadn't been here, Hannah, I might have left and never come back. You showed me there was nothing to be afraid of. Those two didn't have that opportunity."

Essie chuckled. "Can you imagine what their coworkers will say when they read the report? They're likely to get laughed off the force."

"Oh, I hope not! That would be unfair. They're nice people doing their jobs."

Hannah reached over and patted her arm. "No worries. They'll be fine. If they need us to come vouch for them, we can. As I was saying, the ocean is calling my name. I think I'll go change and go for a swim."

"I might join you," Essie said, picking up her dishes. "Last one in is a rotten Easter egg."

Chapter 16

Hannah

Before breakfast the next morning, they'd set the grandfather clock to twelve o'clock in hopes their father could come, but he must have been too busy.

Later, Hannah stood in the living room with her sisters. She walked up to the grandfather clock and set the time to three o'clock. Backing up, she linked arms with her sisters. Slowly, their mother's figure formed in the clock until she stepped into the living room with them. The smile on her face was as broad as the sunrise. "My girls! Together! How I love it!" She gathered them into a huge hug. "Who called me this time?" she asked.

Hannah raised her hand.

Her mother gave her an extra hug. "I'll focus on you this time. But how lovely to see you all again. Things are still good between you?"

"Yes, Mother," Essie said with a shy smile. "Only every now and then we get a little grumpy with each other." She pulled her mother toward the sofa. Hannah and Essie sat on the sofa with their mother.

"I'll get the cookies and milk," Sharon said as she skittered off to the kitchen.

Their mother whispered, "You never go hungry when Sharon's around." They laughed quietly so they wouldn't hurt Sharon's feelings. "Tell me about my grandchildren!"

The day passed quickly. Sharon had the meals already prepared so no effort was spent fixing them. Videocalls with their families allowed them to share a few minutes of their grandmother's time. The sound of a family's laughter filled the living room of the small cottage.

As they focused on the small screen on their mother's lap, one of Essie's children said, "Who's that?" Spinning around, the sisters saw their young, attractive father standing behind the sofa.

"Wow, Grandfather, you're hot!"

"Sylvie!" Essie chided her teenaged daughter. "That's not a nice thing to say."

Her father laughed heartily. "Why, thank you, Sylvie. I don't hear those words too often."

When the call ended, Sharon called Sam who had only a few minutes between classes to talk. Hannah called her boys and Headless. They'd already cleared the air about staying alone with Mrs. Hagg. Surprisingly, the boys didn't complain about it as much as she thought they would. Seems Mrs. Hagg was nicer than the two of them thought. They'd seen her heart.

Afterwards, Hannah sat in the overstuffed chair. The occasions of her family being together were rare, and she fully appreciated the moment. Her father looked like a millennial fresh from the office, neatly groomed in his three-piece suit. It was easy to see why her mother had fallen for him.

Her mother looked much older, yet still a pretty woman. Her playful attitude kept her that way. No wonder her father had fallen for her. She had always been optimistic and cheerful. The only times she uttered a cross word was when she and her sisters weren't getting along.

A question arose Hannah had wondered about. "Father, how did you and Mother meet?" She leaned forward and got another cookie before relaxing on the sofa.

A look passed between her parents showing their love

had not died but had grown stronger in death. "I had a meeting with Mother Nature about a few things I thought she needed to know. As I was going to the villa where she was staying with some of her children, I heard a girl laughing. That beautiful sound came from this woman here. She was a waitress at a restaurant I was walking by. As soon as my meeting was over, I rushed back and got a table where she was my waitress. I spent the afternoon falling in love."

Their mother laughed. "I didn't know I was falling in love with Father Time."

"Have you been married before?" Essie asked her ageless father.

Their father crossed his arms and looked intently at his daughters. "Yes, a few times. Every millennium or so, the Great One shows me a special woman to love. Your mother is one of six through all the millennia." He stroked his goatee and added, "You have siblings who are long dead, and you're cousins to a great many people."

The mood in the room grew somber. "Did you tell Mother you'd never die, but she would?"

"Of course. As your husbands explained it to you. You are mortal. They are not. But you'll have long lives before you join your mother in the beyond."

Hannah said, "It'll be a long while before Essie gets to rest in peace. She'll be back thirteen times to visit her kids."

"I feel shorted with only one child," Sharon said, laughing after she'd said it.

Their parents didn't laugh but exchanged somber glances. "Girls, you're mistaken. The clock is only for your mother. When your last visit is done, I will come and take the clock back with me."

Hannah felt as though the wind has been kicked out of her. "But Mother said to keep the cottage and the clock forever!"

"No, I said to not sell it and hang on to it. Your father built this place for me as a place to raise his children. Even when the clock is gone, the cottage will still be here. You can do what you will with it after it's served its purpose."

The sisters sat still, frozen in place. Sharon was hardly breathing. Essie looked pale, like she was in distress. Hannah felt empty. She'd grown used to the idea of keeping the cottage forever and coming back to see her boys after she passed. That had been snatched away.

Her father looked at his watch and rose from the sofa. "I have to go, but I'm glad to see you all." He hugged his daughters before fading away into the clock.

With arms held wide, her mother waved for her daughters to join her on the sofa. "Don't be sad. It's one of the privileges of being the wife of Father Time but sadly, it doesn't extend to his children."

Hannah wiped a tear away before handing the box of tissues to Essie. "It's okay, Mother. At least we got to see you."

A strip of moonlight lit up Hannah's bedroom as she stirred from her slumber. Feeling more rested than she had in days, she stretched and yawned. Now that the ghosts were gone, they could set the grandfather clock to five before going to bed. Being able to stretch time inside the cottage allowed them to stay there without taking much time from their families. They'd arrive home well rested and ready for normal life.

Hannah sat up in bed and looked around. Something on her nightstand caught her eye. A small wrapped box sat on top of an envelope. Someone had crept in her room last night, and she'd never heard it. An uncomfortable thought. She picked up the items. The handwritten script spelling out her name didn't seem sinister, so she opened it.

The rich ecru stationery was embossed with FT. Inside the message read:

My dearest Hannah,

Having our family together once more was a glimpse back to a time of great happiness. I wish I had been and could be with you more, but alas, my work is too important and too busy for that to occur. In the box is a token of my love that I hope you will always wear close to your heart. It symbolizes the love I have for you, and I hope it will evoke happy memories of our little family. Hold on to it during times of trouble.

With deepest regards and love, Father

Hannah opened the box to find a pendant shaped like the face of the grandfather clock in the living room. She lifted the heavy, yellow gold necklace. The initials HTH were engraved on back. The chain was long enough to allow the pendant to hang by her heart.

Throwing back the covers, Hannah gathered the things and went into the living room. Essie was already there with the necklace around her neck.

"I see you got one too," Essie said as she fingered hers.

Hannah waved her note around. "And a note?"

Essie nodded.

"Me too," Sharon said from the hallway. "I didn't hear him come in. Did you?" She paused for a second, then continued into the kitchen.

Hannah sat in the overstuffed chair. Tissues covered the top of the coffee table where they'd been thrown last night during their post-mother-visit discussion. The tears had flowed freely at the thought of having only one more visit with their mother. After that, she'd be gone forever. And the clock would be too. They'd have no way to get a hold of their father. They'd lose both parents at the same time. They felt the sting of passing time. Crying together brought some comfort.

Before the aroma of coffee entered the living room, Sharon stirred up scrambled eggs and warmed up the last of the coffee cake. The cupboards were now bare, other than the lone container of instant pancake mix and a bottle of syrup just in case of another emergency visit. Little was said during the meal. Individual thoughts were too deep for discussion.

A last swim in the morning ocean washed away the last of Hannah's tension. She'd had a day with her mother. The cottage was peaceful again. Her boys were okay with Mrs. Hagg. All was well.

Her sisters were prepared to go after they'd cleaned and straightened the small cottage. It would be ready for their next visit. Sharon's therapy baking was distributed to homeless shelters, and the rental car had been returned.

Hannah called Headless to set a time for his arrival with the talisman. She liked riding in Santa's sleigh, but the talisman travel was much faster than the reindeer.

After a shower, she zipped her bag and rolled it out to the living room. She hoped she could hang on to the talisman and her bag during transit. She'd get a backpack for her things if she continued to use that mode of travel.

She walked out on the front porch to find her sisters already there. "What are you talking about?" she asked as she sat down and watched them sway slowly in the porch swing.

Essie looked at Hannah. "We've decided—" she pointed to herself and Sharon "—that even though we agreed the three of us would come or none of us would come, it wasn't a good idea. You and Headless could've come to take care of this ghost business without us here. The next time ghosts come intruding, send Headless down. I've had all the ghost interactions I care to have."

Hannah smiled. "Hindsight steers the future. If something comes up, I can come check it out since I'm the closest. Maybe Mrs. Hagg will let us keep the talisman. That way I can pop down easily. I've had my turn calling Mother. You needn't worry whether I'll call her without you here."

A gasp drew Hannah's attention to Sharon. With

lifted eyebrows, her mouth wagged a little before she could say, "I never worried about that. I trust you."

Hannah felt her face flush in the warm breeze. "Thanks. Anyway, I'll call you if something else comes up."

An easy silence settled on the porch like dust. Big fluffy clouds were gathering in a promise for an afternoon shower to clean the air.

Essie sighed. "Only one more time with Mother. Then she's gone forever." She gingerly rubbed the pendant from their father.

Sharon sniffed and held up her bag to her face.

Hannah rubbed her forehead as her shoulders stiffened. When she got home, she'd have Headless give her one of his wonderful massages to relax her. Or being home might help. "We've had more time with her than most people get. I'm thankful for that. Any ideas on when you want to do that?"

Essie shook her head. "Not right now. Sometime that's nowhere near any of our holidays."

That went without saying. Next time, they'd make a planned trip rather than be called to settle some issue or another.

A soft snap was heard inside the cottage. Headless called, "Ready to go home?"

Hannah stood up. "I think our ride home is here." She paused. "I wanted to tell you both, you showed real courage during our ordeal with the captain and his crew. I'm proud of how you managed."

Sharon rolled her eyes. "Please don't ask me to do it again." She laughed loudly, then got up to follow Hannah into the house.

"Me neither!" said Essie, following close behind.

In the middle of the living room stood Headless holding his arms open for his wife. Hannah rushed over to fill the empty space. He gave her a quick peck before saying, "Look what I have!" He reached inside his jacket and pulled out three talismans.

Sharon touched one of them. "We each get one?"

"With one firm condition. No one but your husbands can know about these magic talismans. Mrs. Hagg wanted only you three to know, but I told her there would be too much white lying going on if Easter and Santa didn't know about them. She reluctantly agreed. No sense you getting your names on the naughty list for a stone."

Sharon took one with the expression of someone looking at a valued treasure. "That was nice of her to do that. It wouldn't look good for Mrs. Claus to be naughty. Thank her for saving my reputation."

Essie gingerly took a talisman. "The secret is safe with me. If my kids ever knew about this, I'd never see them again. Thank her for me too. This will save me a lot of worry about how to get here next time. Is there a limit on how many it can transport at a time?"

Headless grimaced. "I forgot to ask, but we'll let you know." He looked at Hannah who was holding his hand. "Ready to go home, honey?"

"In a minute." She locked the door and hugged each of her sisters. Getting her bag, she listened to her sisters say the words and heard the two soft pops as her sisters went home. "Now I'm ready. What were those words again? Pop my bubble, I'm in trouble, take me there on the double. Home. Take me home." And with a snap, they were gone.

About the Author

The author spent her life doing many different things. She's been a wife and mother, a teacher, a statistician, a literacy tutor, timber sale accountant, an archeological technician, and a technical writer/editor. Now retired, she loves to quilt, sew, and write in her home in the Pacific Northwest where she lives with her husband. Her favorite books to read have adventure sprinkled with humor.

She has self-published several novels, one children's book, and a non-fiction book that are available on Kindle and Amazon.

The author's last name is pronounced "care." She hopes that's what everyone will do. Care about each other.

Other Books by C.S. Kjar:

The Treasure of Adonis

Blessings From the Wrong Side of Town

The Five Grannies Go to the Ball

Scraps of Wisdom: All I Needed to Know I
Learned in Quilting Class

The Secrets of the Clock: Book 1 of the
Sisters of Time Series

For more information:

Visit my website at
http://www.cskjar.com
and my Facebook page at
http://www.facebook.com/cskjar.
You can also follow me on Twitter at @cskjar.

Asking a big favor...

One of the best things you can do for an author is write a review. Please tell me what you thought of this novel by leaving a review with one or more of your favorite retailers. Even a short review, one or two lines, can be a tremendous help to me. Your review is also a gift to other readers who may be searching for just this sort of story, and they will be grateful that you helped them find it.

If you write a review, please send me an email at cskjar.books@gmail.com so I can thank you with a personal reply. Also, let me know when you tell your friends, readers' groups, and discussion boards about this book.

Thank you very much for your support. C.S. Kjar

ACKNOWLEDGEMENTS

First and foremost, thanks to my husband who has put up with me all these decades and supports me in my writing career. Thanks to him for my woman cave and my writing desk that lets me sit or stand to write. He's the best.

Thanks also to all those who helped me with this book series. Your encouragement means more than I can say.

The Daughters of Time,

Book 3

The Secrets of the Storm

Three years have passed since Essie Bunny, Sharon Claus, and Hannah Horseman have visited their mother's cottage in Florida. The next visit with their mother will be the last. Forever. Putting it off keeps the anticipation alive.

The storm of the century hits Florida and causes incalculable damage. The sisters check on the fate of the cottage and find ruins. How will they find the clock that will let them see their mother one more time?

Made in the USA
San Bernardino, CA
16 July 2018